THE PASSION OF SACCO AND VANZETTI

A New England Legend

THE PASSION OF SACCO AND VANZETTI

A New England Legend

GREENWOOD PRESS, PUBLISHERS
WESTPORT, CONNECTICUT

The Library of Congress has catalogued this publication as follows:

Library of Congress Cataloging in Publication Data

Fast, Howard Melvin, 1914-
    The passion of Sacco and Vanzetti.

    1. Sacco-Vanzetti case--Fiction. I. Title.
PZ3.F265Pas5 ₍PS3511.A784₎   813'.5'2   72-138227
ISBN 0-8371-5584-3

Originally published in 1953 by The Blue Heron Press, Inc.,
New York

Reprinted with permission.

Reprinted in 1972 by Greenwood Press, Inc.
51 Riverside Avenue, Westport, CT 06880

Library of Congress catalog card number 72-138227
ISBN 0-8371-5584-3

Printed in the United States of America

10 9 8 7 6 5 4 3 2

To THOSE *brave Americans who, today and yesterday, have accepted prison and even death—rather than betray the principles they believed in, the land they loved, or the people whose trust they bore.*

THE PASSION OF SACCO AND VANZETTI

A New England Legend

Prologue

On the 15th of April, in the year 1920, a carefully planned and ruthlessly executed payroll robbery occurred in the town of South Braintree, Massachusetts. In the course of this robbery, a paymaster and a payroll guard were killed by the bandits.

Subsequently, two men, Nicola Sacco, a shoe worker, and Bartolomeo Vanzetti, one-time baker and kiln worker, and now a fish peddler, were arrested and charged with this robbery and murder. They were brought to trial in Dedham, Massachusetts, for murder, and found guilty by the jury which heard the case.

Under Massachusetts law, pleas are heard and motions are presented in such a case before the judge passes sentence. In this, the Sacco and Vanzetti Case, such pleas and motions stretched through a period of seven years. Not until April 9, 1927, did the presiding judge in the case sentence the two men to death, and then he ordered that such sentence should be carried out on the 10th of July, 1927.

However, the execution of this sentence was delayed, for one reason or another, until the 22nd of August, 1927.

Chapter 1

SIX O'CLOCK in the morning is the beginning of the day. If the day begins then, eighteen hours are left until the time called midnight, which, in the minds of so many, is the end of the day.

At six o'clock in the morning, animals and things close to animals smell the day and feel the day, and the fish turn over and show their bellies and look at the cloudy, gray light that falls upon the water. The birds, flying high, can see the lip of the sun, and on the ground, the dust mixes with the morning mist; and rising out of this mist like a medieval castle, is an octagonal-shaped prison.

On the prison walls, the guards who stand watch, turn their somber, thoughtless eyes to the daylight. Soon the roosters will crow, and sunshine will appear upon the earth again. The prison guard is a man like other people. There are thoughts that he thinks, and dreams that he dreams, but he is also aware that a whole history of civilization, an echoing and re-echoing song of the whip, separates him from ordinary people like you and me. And he is different,

13

entrusted with man's best hopes and most frightful fears, which he must guard with his gun and his club.

At this same time of the morning, inside the prison in the death house, a thief awoke. The almost soundless whispering and grunting and creaking of an earth warmed by the first suggestion of daylight, awakened him; and he stretched out on his bunk, and yawned, and felt fear creep through his bones and his blood stream, even as consciousness and awakening came to him.

The name of this man is Celestino Madeiros. He is twenty-five years old, hardly more than a boy, and not uncomely. All the awful years of hate and violence and passion have left less of a mark upon him than they might have. He has a straight nose, a broad, full-lipped mouth, and straight brows. His dark eyes are heavy with fear and longing.

This man is Madeiros, the thief. He comes from sleep into consciousness, and thereby he comes into the knowledge that this is the last day of life that he has upon this earth.

The thought makes him shiver, and cold chills race across his body. Even though it is summer time and warm, he draws the blanket over him in an attempt to stop the chills and to light some fire in his own heart. It does no good, and the chills creep over him again and again. Thus does he awaken, filled with the coldness of fear.

First, Madeiros tried to reassure himself by thinking himself out of this place entirely; he closed his eyes and plunged back into his memories in order that he might believe he was elsewhere, that he was not a full grown man of twenty-five years, that he was once again a school

14

boy in New Bedford, Massachusetts. He thought of his days at school. He saw himself sitting in the room where his teacher taught him arithmetic, which he did well with, for his mind could cope with numbers, and then in another room with another teacher, where he was taught to spell words in the complex language that his mother and father had chosen for him, even as they chose the city of New Bedford, the State of Massachusetts, and the land of America. And here he did poorly, for he could not grapple with these strange words.

The thought of this choice of theirs and of their coming here, plucked him back to prison from his vision of school. Whereupon, he cursed them for not remaining in the Azores, where all their generations had been before they picked up and left and came to America; and when he realized that here and now, on the last day of his life, he was cursing his parents, his father and his beloved mother who had brought him onto the earth, he crawled out of bed and fell upon his knees and began to pray.

The thief prayed for his sins. Of sins he had many, and more than enough. He had drunk and gambled and whored and stolen and killed. He clasped his hands before him, pressed his face upon the bed, and muttered into the bedclothes:

"Mother of God, forgive me for all that I have done. I have sinned all the sins that a man can sin, but I want to be forgiven. All these days and months that I have thought about myself and my fate and what I did and what brought me here, I have seen that some of it was not my own doing. Did I ask to become a companion to sin? The only thing I ever asked was forgiveness. Everything else happened, but forgiveness I asked. I don't want wrong to remain wrong. I tried to right it and to make the wrong right. No one should suffer for me. I confessed my crime. I absolved the two others, the shoemaker and the fish peddler. What more may I do? Did I ask to be born? Did I ask for you to bring me onto this earth? I am here, and I made the best or the worst of it. And now it is finished. I only ask for forgiveness."

Thus he finished his prayer, but even after he finished, he kept muttering his name as if he were seeking to extract a magic spell from it. "I am Celestino Madeiros," he kept saying. And after he had said that over and over at least twenty times, he broke down and put his face in his hands, and wept. He wept very quietly, because he knew it was early in the morning, and he did not want to awaken any of the other prisoners. But if anyone had been there to see it and hear it, they could not have remained unaffected. There was a heartbreaking quality in his great sorrow for himself and for the end he was coming to.

He had been sentenced to die in the electric chair, and tonight the sentence would be carried out. He had lived only twenty-five years, and of these few, a number had been spent in prison; yet for all of that, it was surprising what evil he had managed to crowd into the few short years that had been his.

As a child, he ran wild as an animal, full of hatred, anger and hopelessness, and he grew poorly, twisted and bent, in the dirty back streets, first of New Bedford, Massachusetts, and afterwards, of Providence, Rhode Island. In school he learned little. They thought he was a witless fool, and the other children called him names for the difficulty he had in learning. "Slow-wit—dim-wit—rubber-head," they called him. But the truth of it was that his eyes were bad, and his eyes hurt when he looked too long and too hard at anything.

So he came to avoid school, and he learned other things. He was robbing unguarded warehouses when he was twelve, and freight cars when he was fourteen. At the age of fifteen, he knew the tactics of a pimp, and he abided by the ethics of a procurer. He lived between the pool rooms and the whore houses, and he drank full, long draughts of the civilization which had been provided for him. At seventeen, he had carried out five stick-ups. Half a year later, he killed his first man.

In so many words, this was a thief. What had gone into making the thief was a complex of intricate circumstances that he himself could neither understand nor explain, and which nobody else was particularly interested in explaining. He was there in the ghettos and the alleys; he was part of the scene. When the police picked him up, they beat him because they saw that he was a thief, a fact printed, stamped, and emblazoned on him, and therefore it was evident that he needed to be beaten. Whereupon, he did his best to see to it that the police did not pick him up, and he used what poor skill he had.

Now and again, when a job of honest work came his way, he refused it. He did not know how to work any more than he knew how to live without being a thief. For work he had fear and scorn, and horror and diffidence. So when work came his way, he retreated from it.

Once his pattern was set, everything that happened to him was inevitable. Things happened to him like clockwork, and their happening was the miserable logic of his existence. It was the miserable logic of his existence that sooner or later he should be a part of murder.

It was the miserable logic of his life and existence that, when he was just eighteen years and one month old, they should come to him in Providence where they knew about him. Two men came to him. They were men with cold, hard eyes and evil ways, and they had already said to themselves that he, Celestino Madeiros, was of their own kind. So they came to him and told him about a job they had planned and prepared, and did he want to be in it?

Yes, he said, he wanted to be in it.

There was a lot of money in this job. If he would be in this job, then he would live like a king, with his pockets stuffed full of money, and then he could have dope and liquor and women to his heart's content.

Yes—he would be in on it.

A day after this discussion, on April 15th in the year 1920, this thief, Celestino Madeiros, got into a car with three other men. They drove north from Providence, Rhode Island, to the town of South Braintree in Massachusetts, where they arrived shortly before three o'clock in the afternoon. They parked their car in front of a shoe factory. Inside the shoe factory, a payroll of $15,776.00 was being made up. They knew about this payroll, because they had their contacts inside the factory. Now they parked their car and waited until the payroll make-up was completed, and the two payroll guards came out of the factory, carrying the money in heavy metal boxes. That was just a minute or two before three o'clock. When these two guards appeared, two of the men who were in the car got out of the car and walked over to them and shot them down in cold blood—without even giving them a chance to surrender or run away. The two men picked up the payroll boxes and leaped back into the car, and then the car drove away.

It had been very easy for Madeiros. He only had to sit in the car with his gun ready. He did not have to kill this time. Others did the killing for him. And when the loot was divided, almost three thousand dollars of it was his.

If the life of Celestino Madeiros was inevitable, then his death was just as inevitable. If he escaped one crime, another crime caught up with him. And here he was, seven years later, twenty-five years old, waiting in the death house for his execution.

The terrible irony of it was that on the same day, two more men would be executed, two men who were accused of the double murder at South Braintree—the murder which Madeiros had witnessed, the murder which Madeiros had been an accessory to.

Madeiros knew this. He knew these two men. One of them was a shoe worker whose name was Sacco. The other was a fish peddler whose name was Vanzetti, and both of them were plain Italian workers. Madeiros himself was not Italian, but Portuguese, yet he felt a kinship to these men, and his tight, frightened heart warmed to them. During the years he had spent in prison, he had thought very deeply about these two men who had been sentenced to death for a crime which they did not commit or have anything to do with, but which he himself did commit and did have much to do with. He had thought of many other things while in prison, many things beside this particular crime. It was not easy for him to think. He had no rational basis of knowledge around which to group his thoughts, and therefore the process of thinking was slow and painful, and very often, without any clear meaning or logical conclusion. Perhaps it might be said that what a normal person could think about in a matter of hours, took Madeiros many weeks.

Yet out of this thinking there emerged a glimmer of understanding of his own situation, his own life, his own destiny, and also some comprehension of the irresistible forces which had played upon him and taken him step by step to this terrible ending. Out of his thoughts there had come a degree of pity for himself as well as for others, and sometimes he wept and sometimes he prayed. At one point during an interval of prayer, the realization came to him that he must not allow these two men, Sacco and Vanzetti, to perish for a crime of which they were innocent, but which he himself had committed. Once he understood this, a sort of peace came upon him, a release from tensions within him. And now, so long afterwards, he remembered well the deep serenity with which he wrote out his first confession and tried to send it from jail to a newspaper he sometimes read—the *Boston American*. But instead of reaching the newspaper, the confession was brought to a man called Deputy Sheriff Curtis, who put the letter away, and tried to make that the end of it.

But Madeiros would not let it be the end, and he made a second confession, and this confession he gave to a trusty, and the trusty took it along the rows of cells and handed it to Nicola Sacco. Afterwards, the trusty described to Madeiros how Sacco had read it and how he had begun to tremble after reading it, and then how he had begun to weep, the tears pouring down his face. And when poor, bedeviled Madeiros heard this story, his heart once again swelled with joy, and once again he had that splendid feeling of tranquility and peace.

But many, many months had passed since then. Madeiros did not know all that had transpired after his confession had been made. But he did know that it had not changed a sequence of events already planned, either those events which concerned himself, or those events which concerned Sacco and Vanzetti. All three of them were going to die. He, Celestino Madeiros, for crimes of which he was guilty, and the shoemaker and the fish peddler for crimes of which they were innocent. . . .

The thief finished his prayers and rose to his feet and moved to the tiny window of his cell where he could look out upon the new light of a new day. In the swirling, cloudy mist of morning, he could see no more than an occasional section of the prison wall. But his imagination went beyond that wall, and suddenly and momentarily he experienced a surge of gladness that upon this day he would be set free, and his soul would leap in flight to whatever judgment place awaited it. But this surge of joy was only momentary. It died as it was born, and Madeiros turned back to his bed with cold fear once again his only companion.

He desired to pray again, but he could think of no more prayers which would be either fitting or necessary for him to say. He sat down on his bed and put his face in his hands, and after a little while, he began to weep again. Tears came more easily than prayers.

Chapter 2

THE WARDEN awakened from a dream that was not unfamiliar. There were some dreams that repeated themselves night after night like chronic illness, and in most of them, roles were reversed, and he who was warden became prisoner, and he who was prisoner became warden. Now he woke up into full daylight and sunshine and the glint of blue sky through the window; but the persons and colors and words that were in the dream, remained closer to him for the moment than the reality of his awakening.

In his dream, he always protested the same way. He always felt the same fear, the same terrible frustration. He always argued,

"But I am the Warden."

"That cuts no ice."

"But you don't seem to understand. I am the Warden of this prison."

"It's you who don't understand. As we told you before, that cuts no ice here. None at all. Absolutely none."

"Who are you?"

"That's not to the point, either. To the point is your own situation—to remain quiet and do as you are told. Make no trouble."

"You don't seem to know who you are talking to. You are talking to the Warden. I can come as I please and go as I please. I can leave here any time I want to leave here."

"Oh, no, you can't. You can't leave here any time you want to leave here. You can't leave here at all."

"Of course I can."

"These are your own delusions of grandeur. Grandeur has nothing at all to do with this, and we will not tolerate your delusions. You are here in a prison. You do as you are told. Button your lip, mind the orders, and do as you are told, and you'll get along."

That was the usual flow of the dialogue. They never believed that he was the Warden. It didn't matter how much he pleaded or reasoned or argued or produced this evidence or that evidence to document his position. They in turn could produce their evidence. In his dreams once, he had been asked,

"Who decides to be or plans to be or dreams of being a jail guard, a turnkey, or even a warden? Who? A child wants to be a fireman, a policeman, a soldier, a doctor, a lawyer, a driver of a four-horse team—but who on God's earth ever wanted to be a jail guard or a warden?"

Awake, the Warden reflected upon the deep truth of this particular challenge of his dream. At moments when he pitied himself, it seemed to him that people who worked in prisons were wind-tossed people who arrived at a destination that was never of their own choice. This morning he wanted to believe this. He awakened with a woeful feeling of emptiness. Somewhere in his sleep, along the way, he had lost something; and there would be no finding it today. He tried to tell himself that today was a day he had neither made nor ordered.

With such thoughts, he sat up in his bed, put his feet into his slippers, and went to clean himself and shave, and make himself look like what a warden should look like. He gargled and he combed his hair, and all the while, he conducted an argument with himself, telling himself that this was not his doing. In the course of that kind of thing, he had a sudden realization that each and every person connected with the executions today must be saying the same thing; that each absolved himself. His own absolution was a middle matter. He was neither the most important nor the least important person concerned. He had been the Warden before today, and unquestionably he would be the Warden after today. Things would quiet down a little. One had to remember that people possessed the facility to forget. They could forget anything on earth. Never was a lover born who in time could not forget his own true love, and that notwithstanding how true the love was. The Warden, to some extent at least, was a philosopher. This was an affliction of the trade, an occupational disease. He knew that all wardens were philosophers. Like old sea captains, the very ark they ruled gave them a dignity at odds with the crew and passengers they carried.

"Well," he said to himself on this particular morning, "it's no use going on thinking that way. Here's today which had to come, and in time it will be over. The thing to do is to get about it and see that everything is all right, and

24

make things as easy and comfortable as they can be made."

He finished dressing, and decided that he would take a look at the death house before he had his breakfast. He walked across the yard and was greeted by the captain of the guards, and even by a trusty or two who were already about their work. The morning life of the prison he ruled had begun. Metal doors clanged open and rolled shut. Prisoners came by, pushing hand trucks full of laundry. The clatter of pots and dishes, a whole bustle of activity, went on around the kitchen and bakery doors, and already, corridors were being mopped, swabbed down, washed with gray lye-impregnated water. At this time of the morning, a little past seven o'clock, the prisoners were going to their morning meal. The Warden heard the regimental tread of their feet, the chopping sound of half a thousand men moving in rhythm, of a thousand leather shoes slapping the concrete. A little later, the sound of trays and spoons came to him through walls and along cell blocks. His ears were marvelously tuned to all the various sounds and noises of the prison, for these were the sounds and noises of his life. In that sense at least, his dream was most deeply true. He lived his whole life in jail.

Now he came to the death house. He chose Vanzetti to speak to, and that was natural, for it was never difficult to speak to Vanzetti. He walked up to Vanzetti's cell, rubbing his hands together, cheerful, brisk, business-like, determined that he would not make any funereal occasion out of this, but would go at it straightforwardly and directly, with no fuss or bother.

Vanzetti, who had been sitting on his bed, fully dressed, rose to meet the Warden, and they shook hands gravely.

"Good morning, Bartolomeo," the Warden said. "I am very pleased to see you looking well. I am, indeed."

"Perhaps better than I feel."

"You couldn't be expected to feel very good. In your place, no one would feel very good."

"I suppose that's true," Vanzetti nodded. "I don't suppose that you think too much before you say something like that, but that doesn't change it. It remains a very true thing. So often, there are things that you say in such a fashion without thinking too much about them, and they remain very true and very direct."

The Warden observed him with interest. The Warden understood that if he himself were in Vanzetti's place, he could not have behaved in this way. He would have been very afraid, very frightened, his voice would have choked up, his throat would have tightened, his skin would have become wet, and he would have trembled from head to foot. The Warden knew himself, and he knew that beyond a shadow of a doubt, this was the case with him; but it was not the case with Vanzetti. Vanzetti seemed quite calm. His deep-set eyes looked at the Warden appraisingly. His heavy mustache added a quizzical note to his appearance, and his strong, high-boned, melancholy face seemed to the Warden no different from what it had been at any other time.

"Have you seen Sacco yet this morning?" Vanzetti asked the Warden.

"Not yet. I will see him a little later."

"I am worried about him. He is very weak because of the hunger strike. He is sick. I worry a good deal about him."

"I worry about him, too," the Warden said.

"Yes, of course. Anyway, I think you should see him and speak to him."

"All right, I'll do that. What else would you like me to do?"

Suddenly, Vanzetti smiled. He looked at the Warden suddenly as a grown, mature man would smile at a child.

"Do you really want to know what I would like you to do?" Vanzetti asked.

"What I can do," the Warden answered. "I can't do everything. Whatever I can do, Bartolomeo, I will be very happy to do. Today you have some privileges. You can have whatever you want to eat. You can have the Priest whenever you want him."

"I would like to spend some time with Sacco. Can you arrange that? There is a great deal that I want to say to him, but somehow it has never been said. If you can arrange for me to spend some time with him, a few hours, I would be very grateful for that."

"I think that can be arranged. I will try. But don't be disappointed if it can't be."

"You must understand, it is not because I am stronger or braver than he is. Perhaps I am able to give that impression. But the appearance is a superficial one. Inside, he is as strong as I am, and braver than I am."

"You are both very brave and good people," the Warden said. "I am terribly sorry that all this has to happen."

"There is nothing you can do about it. It wasn't your fault."

"Anyway, I'm sorry," the Warden said, "and I regret it. I wish it could be different."

The Warden didn't want to talk any more. There was nothing more he could think of saying, and he also realized that this kind of talk was having a profoundly upsetting effect upon him. He asked Vanzetti to excuse him, explaining that today was a day when he had a great many things to do, more than he would usually have. Vanzetti appeared to understand.

When the Warden sat down to breakfast—usually he ate a fairly large breakfast, but this morning he had no appetite at all—he was struck with the conviction that today, as had happened several times in the past, indeed, only a week ago, the execution would be postponed; and neither Sacco nor Vanzetti would die. He realized that even if this did happen, there would still be the execution of the thief, Celestino Madeiros; and while that would be painful and unpleasant, it would certainly not be as upsetting to his nerves as this particular business with Sacco and Vanzetti.

Having made this observation to himself, the Warden felt a good deal better, and the more he speculated on the possibility, the more it seemed that this would be the case. His whole demeanor changed. He became cheerful, and he smiled for the first time that morning as he observed to his wife that, in his opinion, the execution would be postponed.

He was the sort of man who had, over a period of years, suppressed his own excitement, for the particular events of his life gave no joy to excitement, and little fulfillment to anticipation. His wife, therefore, was rather surprised at the eager note in his voice and at the certainty with which he made this pronouncement. She asked him an obvious question,

"But why should they postpone it any further?"

The answer to this question, which leaped immediately into his mind, gave him reason to pause and to consider the entire proposition. He had intended to say, "The execution will be postponed because it is quite obvious to anyone who knows anything about this case, that these two men are innocent."

But he hesitated to say this, even to his wife. He was unwilling to place himself directly on record with such an observation. He had said too many times that questions of guilt and innocence were not for him or for any warden to decide; therefore, he reviewed some of the aspects of the case, and reminded his wife that there were a number of reasonable doubts as to the guilt of the two men.

"But how can anyone survive this kind of thing?" his wife wondered. "For seven years it has been going on like this—death and reprieve, death and reprieve. I don't know but that it wouldn't be better to finish with it. I couldn't live that way."

"Where there's life, there's hope," the Warden said.

"I don't understand," his wife went on. "Everyone connected with this thinks so well of these men."

"They are very nice men. You would have to go a long distance to find two men like them. I can't explain it. They are very nice and very gentle men. They are very quiet, very polite. There has never been a harsh word from either of them. They are not angry at me. I asked Vanzetti about that, and he explained that he understood, and so did Sacco, that it wasn't my fault, what had happened to them. Vanzetti feels that anger is wasted unless it is directed in the right place."

"That's what makes it so strange," his wife said.

"Why is it so strange? This is just the way it is. They are very nice."

"Anarchists," his wife began, "are supposed to—"

"Neither of us knows anything about anarchists when you come right down to it," the Warden interrupted. "This has nothing to do with their being anarchists or not being anarchists. I don't know much about anarchists or communists or socialists. Sacco and Vanzetti may be all three. They may be soaked in evil from head to foot. All I am saying is that you don't notice this when you talk to them. Whenever you talk to them, you come away saying to yourself that these are two men who never, under any conceivable set of circumstances could have committed murder. Anyway, not the kind of murder that they have been accused of committing. That kind of murder is the work of cold-blooded gunmen who shoot down men as if they are dogs. These two men are very different. I don't know just how to put it, but these two men are very tender toward life. They couldn't kill in just that way. Now mind you, I am saying this privately. I say this off the record. If I don't know a murderer, who would?"

"There are all kinds of murderers," his wife reminded him.

"Well, there you go. There you are. I don't blame you. It's like everybody else. You have to keep asking yourself how this can happen to someone who is innocent. When you come right down to it, that is the thing, isn't it?"

"I suppose so," his wife agreed.

"Well, I went to see Vanzetti this morning, and there he

was, just as calm and quiet and as pleasant as if today was like any other day."

At this point in their conversation, they were interrupted by a prison guard who told the Warden that Madeiros was screaming with hysteria, and would the Warden permit the physician to use a few grains of morphine? The Warden excused himself to his wife, wiped his mouth hurriedly, and went along with the guard. They passed by the infirmary and picked up the physician, and the three of them went to Madeiros' cell. When they were still quite a distance from it, they heard the screams, which increased in volume and intensity as they neared the cell.

Madeiros was in the death house, very close by to both Sacco and Vanzetti. In order to reach his cell, the Warden had to pass the cells of both these men; but now he did not bother to peer into the little windows of the death cells to see what the two men were doing.

Madeiros himself lay upon the floor of his cell, his body twitching and writhing spasmodically. In his case, there was a history of epilepsy, and this was not the first fit of this kind he had undergone since being in prison. The Warden tried to speak to him, but he was beyond hearing; he screamed and beat his hands upon the stone floor. A mixture of blood and saliva ran out of his mouth, and the sight of him and the sound of his screaming made the Warden quite sick.

"Now, now, it will be all right," the Warden tried to tell him. "Just take it easy, and here we are and you are not alone any more and it's going to be all right and you might as well calm down and take it easier than this."

31

"It's no use to talk to him," the physician said. "The best thing for me to do is to give him morphine. Do you agree to that?"

"Well, go ahead," the Warden said. "What are you waiting for? Go ahead."

He and the guard held Madeiros while the doctor injected the morphine. In just a few minutes the young man's body relaxed; the hard cords of his muscles began to loosen, and his screaming turned to sobbing.

The Warden left the cell. He felt sick to his stomach. His previous certainty that there would be a delay in the executions today as there had been in the past, now disappeared, and instead, he felt quite sure that today they would go through with it. This was only the beginning of a terrible day. It was only eight o'clock in the morning. He didn't see how he was going to get through the rest of a day like this.

Chapter 3

IT IS SURPRISING how suddenly people became curious about Sacco and Vanzetti and wanted to know something about them, who they were and what they were like. It is also surprising how few people knew about them before the time came for Sacco and Vanzetti to die.

The year 1927 was a strange year, a year for news; and the headlines in the daily press came hard and furious and one on top of the other. It was the midst of the best of all possible times, and Charles A. Lindberg flew the Atlantic Ocean for the first time, one man alone, so that the Baltimore *Sun* was able to cry out, "He has exalted the race of man." Peaches Browning and her aging husband, Daddy Browning, also exalted the race of man, and then Chamberlain and Levine flew the ocean, and Jack Dempsey fought Sharkey before he was defeated by Gene Tunney.

Sacco and Vanzetti, however, were either communists or socialists or anarchists or deeply subversive elements of one kind or another, and there were many newspapers throughout the country that printed never a word about them until the time came for them to die. Even the great journals in Boston and New York City and Philadelphia carried only an occasional line about the case. It had been so long since the case began!

"After all," these newspapers could have said in their own defense, "the Sacco-Vanzetti case began in 1920, and here it is 1927."

The imminence of death made a shoemaker and a fish peddler eloquent; their very silence was eloquent. From early in the morning, very early indeed, on the 22nd of August, the sound and the smell and the scent and the feeling of death were in the air. It would seem, indeed, more than passing strange that in a world where so many hundreds and thousands died unsung and unwept, the death of two agitators and a common thief would make such a commotion and grow into a thing of such tremendous importance. As curious as that was, it was nevertheless the case, and people had to take note of it.

All the newspapers knew what their headlines would be on the following morning, but they needed more than headlines. A reporter, thereupon, went this morning to the place where the family of Sacco lived. Here was the mother of two children, the wife of Sacco. The reporter had been told that many people were interested in Vanzetti, but even more were interested in Nicola Sacco. The case of Nicola Sacco was one of human interest, and anyone who missed that was a fool. Here was Sacco, only thirty-six years old as he stood at the edge of the great, yawning gulf of predetermined death—being one of those singled out to know the very moment of his departure from the earth.

The newspaper man was informed that, according to the simple thoughts of millions of simple folk in this country, Nicola Sacco left behind him great riches, for he was a family man.

Sacco had a wife and two children. His wife's name was Rosa. The boy, who was almost fourteen years old, was named Dante. The little girl, who wasn't yet seven years old, was named Ines. The reporter, given to understand that here was a human interest story of the highest type, was instructed to see the mother of Sacco's children. He must find out how the mother felt and how the children felt.

This particular assignment did not please him, and that was not an extraordinary thing; for even if this reporter had been as hard as flint, such an assignment would not have been an easy one to contemplate. But he had his job to do, and he went on it early, for a complete *beat*, a story that no one else would have before him, knocking at the door of the place where Rosa Sacco lived, at eight o'clock in the morning.

The mother came to the door and opened it and asked him what he wanted. He looked at her, and he had a rather unusual reaction.

"My God!" he said to himself. "Isn't she beautiful! Isn't she one of the most beautiful women I have ever laid eyes on!"

It was very early in the morning. Her hair, tied together hastily, was uncombed, and she had no paint or rouge on her face. Perhaps she was not as beautiful as the reporter felt. He had been prepared for something else. She astonished him with the simple directness of her brown eyes, the awful tranquility of her terribly sad face. Like a cup flowing over, sorrow filled her and poured out. This morning, in the eyes and imagination of the reporter, the grief equated itself with beauty; and this was so disturbing that the reporter experienced an enormous urge to run away. But that was the terror of suddenly revealed truth. His trade was not to deal with truth, but still and all, his trade fed him. Whereupon, he stood there and pursued his inquiries.

"Please go away," the mother said. "I have nothing to say."

He tried to explain to her that he could not go away. Didn't she understand that here was his job, and that possibly his job was the most important in the whole world?

She did not understand that. She told him that her children were still asleep. Speaking painfully, each word embedded in grief, she begged him not to wake the children.

"I don't want to wake them," he said in his defense. "Of all things, I have no desire to wake your children. Can't I come inside for a moment?"

She sighed and shrugged and nodded her head and let him come inside.

The first thing he saw in that house were the sleeping children. Afterwards, it struck him that they were all he saw. He was a very young man, and he was not supposed to have sensitivity to the children of an Italian shoemaker. He himself was a Yankee American, and the child of real honest-to-God Yankees. Not only had he been born in Boston, but his grandfather had been born in Boston, and his great-grandfather had been born in Plymouth, Massachusetts, and his great-great-grandfather had been born in Salem, Massachusetts.

Nevertheless, he saw how a little girl sleeps. There is a singularity in this; in the whole world, nothing else is just like it. A little girl who is not yet seven years old is, in her sleep, the model for all the dreams of angels men have dreamed. This little girl lay with her dark hair spread out above her, her arms outflung, and her face reposeful in its tranquil innocence. Not even a bad dream seemed to disturb her early on this morning. She had her fill of bad dreams already in the past, and perhaps she had dreamed them all out. She had dreamed of an electric chair; she dreamed of it in her own childish way.

She saw, in her dream, a chair with a great frame of electric lights over it, so the whole chair glowed and sparkled with brilliance, and in this chair her father sat, Nicola Sacco. This creation of her childish mind was the result of all her terrible grappling with the vague and frightening two-word image that seeped into her consciousness, heard surreptitiously, heard by accident, heard from other children who used it in mockery. It never occurred to her, of course, to inquire as to the particular ethics of a State which pays no heed to a little girl in relation to a thing like an electric chair.

Hunger strike was just as difficult for her to comprehend, and her dreams had taken other forms for this awful thing. She dreamed of being hungrier than she ever actually was in her real waking life. Once when she was dreaming such a bad dream of overwhelming hunger, she woke up, weeping. That was a night when her mother had not been with her, and her brother Dante rocked her in his arms

37

and comforted her and tried to explain to her that this image which she had evoked was not how such things really happened.

"See," he said to her, "I have a letter from papa which tells all about it."

Then he promised to read her the letter the following day, and of course he did so. She sat with her legs bent and her knees tucked into the circle of her arms, while her brother read the letter her father had written. Thus he read:

"My Dear Son and Companion:

"Since the day I saw you last I had always the idea to write you this letter, but the length of my hunger strike and the thought I might not be able to explain myself, made me put off all this time.

"The other day, I ended my hunger strike and just as soon as I did that I thought of you to write to you, but I find that I did not have enough strength and I cannot finish it at one time. However, I want to get it down in any way before they take us again to the death-house, because it is my conviction that just as soon as the court refuses a new trial to us they will take us there. And between Friday and Monday, if nothing happens, they will electrocute us right after midnight, on August 22nd. Therefore, here I am, right with you with love and with open heart as ever I was yesterday.

"If I stopped hunger strike the other day, it was because there was no more sign of life in me. Because I protested with my hunger strike yesterday as today I protest for life and not for death.

38

"Son, instead of crying, be strong, so as to be able to comfort your mother, and when you want to distract your mother from the discouraging soulness, I will tell you what I used to do. To take her for a long walk in the quiet country, gathering wild flowers here and there, resting under the shade of trees, between the harmony of the vivid stream and of the gentle tranquility of the mothernature, and I am sure that she will enjoy this very much, as you surely would be happy for it. But remember always, Dante, help the weak ones that cry for help, help the prosecuted and the victim, because that are your better friends; they are the comrades that fight and fall as your father and Bartolo fought and fell yesterday for the conquest of the joy of freedom for all and the poor workers. In this struggle of life you will find more love and you will be loved.

"Much I thought of you when I was lying in the deatn-house—the singing, the kind tender voices of the children from the playground, where there was all the life and the joy of liberty—just one step from the wall which contains the buried agony of three buried souls. It would remind me so often of you and your sister Ines, and I wish I could see you every moment. But I feel better that you did not come to the death-house so that you could not see the horrible picture of three lying in agony waiting to be electrocuted, because I do not know what effect it would have on your young age. But then, in another way if you were not so sensitive it would be very useful to you tomorrow when you could use this horrible memory to hold up to the world the shame of the country in this cruel persecution and unjust death. Yes, Dante, they can crucify our bodies today as they are doing, but they cannot destroy our ideas, that will remain for the youth of the future to come.

"Dante, I say once more to love and be nearest to your mother and the beloved ones in these sad days, and I am sure that with your brave heart and kind goodness they will feel less discomfort. And you will also not forget to love me a little for I do—O, Sonny! thinking so much and so often of you.

"Best fraternal greetings to all the beloved ones, love and kisses to your little Ines and mother. Most hearty affectionate embrace.

Your Father and Companion

"P.S. Bartolo send you the most affectionate greetings. I hope that your mother will help you to understand this letter because I could have written much better and more simple, if I was feeling good. But I am so weak."

Even though the little girl did not understand all of the letter, and even though her brother mercifully omitted some, enough remained to bewilder her. Out of this bewilderment, she tried to form a few words of her own to send him.

The turmoil of thought injected by this, hardly began to settle, when she received her own letter, addressed to her, with this salutation: "My dear Ines." And then her father went on to talk to her. Each word of the letter meant that her father was talking to her. These were his words:

"I would like that you should understand what I am going to say to you, and I wish I could write you so plain, for I long so much to have you hear all the heart-beat eagerness of your father, for I love you so much and you are the dearest little beloved one.

"It is quite hard indeed to make you understand in your young age, but I am going to try from the bottom of my heart to make you understand how dear you are to your father's soul. If I cannot succeed in doing that, I know that you will save this letter and read it over in future years to come and you will see and feel the same heart-beat affection as your father feels in writing to you.

"It was the greatest treasure and sweetness in my struggling life that I could have lived with you and your brother Dante and your mother in a neat little farm, and learn all your sincere words and tender affection. Then in the summer-time to be sitting with you in the home nest under the oak tree shade—beginning to teach you of life and how to read and write, to see you running, laughing, crying and singing through the verdant fields picking the wild flowers here and there from one tree to another, and from the clear, vivid stream to your mother's embrace.

"I know that you are good and surely you love your mother, Dante, and all the beloved ones—and I am sure that you love me also a little, for I love you much and then so much. You do not know, Ines, how often I think of you every day. You are in my heart, in my vision, in every angle of this sad walled cell, in the sky and everywhere my gaze rests.

"Meantime, give my best paternal greetings to all the friends and comrades, and doubly so to our beloved ones. Love and kisses to your brother and mother.

"With the most affectionate kiss and ineffable caress

from him who loves you so much that he constantly thinks of you. Best warm greetings from Bartolo to you all.

Your Father"

While he talked to her, she closed her eyes and tried to see his face and the motion of his lips, and the twinkle that had sometimes appeared in his eyes even when she saw him in prison.

That, however, was in the past. By the calendar of grown-up people, it was only a few days in the past, but by this little girl's own passage of time and her own calculations for estimating the passage of time, it was a long, long while in the past. Now on this morning, she slept peacefully and gently with the dreams, with the memories, bitter or sweet.

"Please go away," the mother pleaded with the reporter.

The young man looked at the two children again, and then he left. He was not able to remain any longer. He left, and walked away down the road and tried to compose in his mind the little bit that he had seen in such a manner that it would make a story. He was plagued and troubled by many, many things that had come into his consciousness all of a sudden and that were in large measure beyond his understanding.

Never before had he felt the necessity to comprehend what motivated a poor fish peddler and a hard-working shoemaker who were both of them anarchists or communists or something of the sort. Such people came from elsewhere into the edge of his world. They embarked upon motion, and that motion might end in violent death or prison or starvation or the electric chair; but such an

42

ending was expressly reserved for such people. It was no part of his own world and no business of his conscience.

Now it had abruptly become a part of his world and the business of his conscience. He had once taken a girl on a date and boyishly boasted to her of the many experiences that a newspaper man had. This was without question such an experience as he had boasted of. Would he ever tell this experience to anyone in such a boastful, boyish way, he wondered? Certainly, if he could tell it to anyone, then he could make a story of it as he now had to.

But what would the story be? He sensed somehow vaguely and to a degree tragically, that a story beyond any he had ever discovered or told, lay in the tranquil and beautiful faces of the sleeping children. His education told him that "Dante" was the name of an Italian poet, even though he had never read Dante the poet. But he wondered how the Italian shoemaker had come to name his little girl Ines. Such wondering was replaced by the realization that this child must have been born and seen her time of life and growth, all of her time of life and growth, during the seven years which Nicola Sacco and Bartolomeo Vanzetti had spent in prison. This realization came as a most profound shock to the newspaper man, and indeed moved him more than anything which had happened to him that morning.

He was different, and he would never again be as he had been before. Bitter change had begun to fester. He had come too close to death—and thereby too close to life— and it had taken his youth from him.

43

Chapter 4

AT TEN MINUTES to nine, on the morning of August 22nd, the Professor, who was also one of the noted lawyers of the Commonwealth, crossed the lawn toward the Law School building where he would conduct the sixth and last lecture of the series he was giving for the summer session. It was the first time he had ever taught in the summer session, and all through the uncomfortable summer weeks, he found himself torn between a desire for a real vacation in the mountains or at the seashore, and a feeling of relief that he could, after all, be here in Boston, seeing, watching and observing the final developments in the case of Sacco and Vanzetti.

Only rarely did he allow himself to admit, even to himself, how much this case meant to him; and this was because there was a certain danger in admitting this fact— even to himself. When, however, he was provoked by one thing or another into accepting the Sacco-Vanzetti case as a central force in his present day to day existence, his anger at certain forces would become almost uncontrollable. This, perhaps, disturbed him more than anything else. Ever since he had been a young man, he had set his face solidly and determinedly against uncontrollable anger in any situation.

Yet on this special and tranquil and particularly tragic morning, his anger was present, but latent, like a steel spring compressed within him. Only the evening before, he had heard that the President of the University where he taught, who was also the head of an advisory committee inquiring into this case, had connected him with it in a singularly unpleasant fashion.

The President of the University had referred to him, the Professor, as "that Jew," and had gone on to say that there was a little more than met the eye in the eagerness of Jews to leap to the defense of "two Italian communists."

There was nothing either new or particularly revealing in the knowledge that the President of the University did not like Jews. Ever since he had come to the university, the Professor had been acutely aware of the fact that the President of the University had a most pointed dislike for Jews. It must be added that the President of the University practiced an equal dislike for most other minorities of the United States; if his dislike for Jews was more frequently and sharply expressed, it was only because the gates of the university could be less easily closed against Jews than against certain other groups.

The Professor, hurrying across the lawn, was acutely aware of all these things—just as he was most acutely aware of his own appearance.

That awareness rode him with a spur, constantly pricking his sensitivity. All things that the President of the University was, this Professor of Criminal Law was not. The Professor was not a Yankee; he was not even a native-born American; and he was neither blue-eyed nor aristocratic in his bearing. When he spoke, a trace of foreign accent clung to his speech. His dark, piercing, narrow eyes hid themselves behind heavy glasses, and his big head hung loosely from his shoulders. Even if he could have exorcised his own awareness of his appearance, life in Boston in 1927 would not have permitted it.

"Very well," he said to himself this morning as he crossed the lawn. "I march forward as a Jew. Now, this Jew will do a brave or a stupid thing and deliver his last lecture of a series, and the subject will be the case of Sacco and Vanzetti."

This decision, which he had made the evening before, comforted him and also fed fuel to his anger. It was common knowledge on the faculty of the university that the brilliant, penetrating and devastating essay which this Professor had written in defense of Sacco and Vanzetti, and had caused to be published, was hotly resented by the President of the University. Not only did the President consider the Professor's action unwise; but he felt that in taking this action, the Professor of Criminal Law had taken a position, personally as well as publicly, in opposition to the position of the President. The President of the University had his own philosophy of the situation. From his point of view, he saw the power of two naked and disarmed agitators who waited for their death, yet were able to arouse half the world in their defense. This mysterious power terrified him. He could not have comprehended that the Professor of Criminal Law, with whom he was so annoyed, saw nothing of the sort in the two agitators, no such power, but only two terribly forsaken men who waited for their doom.

As the Professor entered the Law School building on this morning, he found three reporters waiting for him. They immediately asked him whether it was true, as was rumored, that this, his last lecture in the *Williams Series,* would be devoted to the Sacco-Vanzetti case?

"It is true," he snapped at them, neither cordial nor expansive.

"Would you care to make any statement, Professor, regarding this lecture or the findings of the special advisory committee?" They referred to the committee headed by the President of the University—and appointed by the Governor, to inquire, as a board of last resort, into the Sacco-Vanzetti case.

"I have no statement to make," the Professor retorted. "If you wish to hear my lecture, you may come into the lecture room. I will not bar the doors to you, but I have no statement to make.'"

The invitation was a generous one, and they followed him into the lecture room. Already, some three hundred students had gathered, an almost complete attendance. His lectures were very well attended for a summer course. It was the same incisiveness and ironical wit that made him so feared and disliked by some, that also won him admiration from others.

"At any rate," he thought to himself as he took his place on the podium, "the students do not abhor me."

He leaned upon the speaker's stand and let his eyes flow over the eager young faces. This lecture hall was one of

47

those old fashioned classrooms built in the amphitheater style. He stood at the bottom of a pit, and around him, climbing all the way up to the ceiling in the rear, were rows of students sitting on the old benches, their pads out and ready for notes, some of them with their chins cradled in their hands, their eyes earnest and eager.

At any rate, he reflected, he had never committed the sin of dullness, and if he had an unyielding penchant for destroying himself, he did at least evoke some excitement from life in the process. Perhaps the President of the University, who had always so carefully eschewed excitement, found that as irritating as the other qualities the Professor exhibited. Now, however, it did not matter; for in all the Professor's thinking about the case of Sacco and Vanzetti, and his own position in relation to this case, he had come to a number of most important conclusions.

At first the Professor was faced with the question of taking a position on the case, any position; a position which said that the two were guilty; a position which denied that the agitators were guilty; or even a position which granted that perhaps certain incidents of the trial were regrettable. For months and months, he had grappled with this tantalizing and disturbing question, whether or not to take a position, whether or not to face the danger of being linked with reds and possibly being called a red himself, and finally, out of his grappling and soul-searching, there had come the determination to inquire into the facts of the case in the fullest possible manner.

He remembered well when he had reached his initial conclusion and made his initial decision, because implicit in that first conclusion was all that flowed from it. His inquiry had been a careful and exhaustive one. He might have intended to dip into the case of Sacco and Vanzetti with only casual interest; the actual result of his decision was to immerse himself in it, and thereby face the need for a second critical decision, asking himself, "Are they guilty, or are they innocent?"

When he had answered that question, he more quickly took the next step. The consequences implicit filled him with fear for many days and weeks. He had fought hard for all the success that was his, and in the course of this struggle, he had faced the necessity of conquering a new land, a new tongue, a new people, a new shame, a new contempt; and all of these things, he had conquered.

When he made his decision he knew full well that he might be surrendering all he had won and achieved; nevertheless, he said to himself quite plainly and forthrightly, "It is too difficult to live in the world as a lie. A lie can exist as a man, but it makes me uncomfortable. Perhaps in time I would have been a very important judge or a very rich lawyer. What I will be now, I have no notion whatsoever, but I will be less uncomfortable."

Whereupon, he sat down and wrote his essay on the Sacco and Vanzetti case.

All of this he remembered now as he looked at the youthful faces and composed his thoughts and arranged his notes, so that he might begin his lecture. He looked up at the clock over the door, and noticed that it was now just one minute after nine o'clock. He cleared his throat, nodded his big head, and tapped with the point of his pencil upon the speaker's stand.

"So we begin," he said, "the last of our lectures concerning the theory of evidence. Over the past weeks, we have dealt with a number of cases taken from what one might call the legal hall of fame—sometimes infamy. All of these cases belong to the past. Today, however, I presume to discuss a case which belongs to the present. The fact that today is the twenty-second of August, makes this particular situation, as well as this case I have chosen, a most important matter. Today is the day appointed by the Governor of this Commonwealth for the execution of Sacco and Vanzetti, the two Italian agitators who await their end in prison in the death house.

"To discuss the evidence upon which these two men were convicted, so few hours before their sentence of death is carried out, might be considered by some as a tactless and impermissible procedure. However, I have not embarked upon this course thoughtlessly, and I consider it neither tactless nor impermissible. A study of history must deal with the living as well as the dead. A good lawyer is a man consciously a part of the motion of history.

"It is also particularly fitting that such a discussion be the concluding section of what has been known as the *Roger Williams Memorial Series*. All too often we take and accept a name with neither a memory of its past nor any particular inquiry into its origin. But it is precisely because Roger Williams dedicated his life to resistance against any interference, whether by the laws of the Church or the State, with the conscience of men, that he has been remembered and will be remembered so long as this country shall endure. This places a certain responsibility upon anyone who presumes to take part in these Williams lectures. Freedom of conscience is more than a dead phrase. It is a living way of life which must be fought for relentlessly and unremittingly. Terrible hazards lie in the path of anyone who embarks upon this struggle for human dignity; however, the rewards are commensurate with the venture.

"Today is not like other days. It is like no other day which I can remember in my life. Today is a day which has been singled out to be remembered and to be made memorable by a sad blow against all who love justice and believe truly in man's freedom of conscience. Thereby, what I am going to say to you today assumes special importance."

The Professor looked around the lecture room now, letting his eyes travel from face to face. Almost every one there gave some evidence of the sense of urgency and crisis which he had communicated to them. He had also communicated an additional factor to himself, for he was tense all over, and he could feel the moisture oozing out of his skin. He knew from experience that before he finished lecturing, he would be soaked with sweat, tired, used up. He began to speak now quite slowly, almost haltingly.

"I wish to begin by reviewing some of the facts of this case. We cannot, of course, in the time allotted to us, have a full recapitulation of it. However, I am sure that you have not remained uninformed on this matter. Our problem here is to consider the events in the light of certain rules and practices of evidence. This, we will attempt to do.

"As you know, the events which led to this pending execution, began a little more than seven years ago, on the fifteenth of April, in the year 1920, in the town of South

Braintree, Massachusetts. At that time, Parmenter, a paymaster, and Berardelli, who was the paymaster's guard, were shot and killed by two armed men. The weapons used were pistols. The paymaster and the guard were carrying two boxes which contained the payroll of the shoe factory of Slater and Morrill, which payroll amounted to $15,776.51. When the double murder occurred, the money was being carried from the shoe company's office building to the factory, along the main street. Simultaneously with the murder, a car containing two other men, approached and halted at the spot, whereupon the thieves threw the payroll money into the car, leaped in, and drove away at high speed. After two days had passed, this car which had been used in the robbery, was found abandoned in the woods some distance from South Braintree; and the police discovered tracks of a smaller car leading away from that spot. In other words, a separate car had met the murder car, taken on the criminals, and driven them away to safety.

"At this very time, the police were investigating a crime of like nature in the town of Bridgewater, not far away. The two crimes were linked by the fact that, in each case, a car was used, and in each case, observers expressed the opinion that the criminals were Italians.

"Thereby, we have before us a situation where the police do have certain clues as to the perpetrators of a crime; they are looking for an Italian who owns a car; since in one of these crimes, the Bridgewater crime, the car had driven away in the direction of Cochesett, the police accepted the not unreasonable assumption that the Italian who owned the car might be living in that town.

"I must interpose at this point, the fact that such a presumption would have been applicable to any New England industrial town; since there is no industrial town in this state which does not have a considerable Italian population, and since the very law of averages guarantees that at least one of the Italian residents would own a car. But this did not deter the police, who discovered in Cochesett, an Italian named Boda, who owned such a car.

"Eliminating some of the details, we come to a garage owned by one Johnson, where Boda's car was found—having been brought there for repairs. The police instituted a watch, to determine who would call for the car. On the night of May fifth, about three weeks after the original crime, Boda and three other Italians did, in fact, call.

"At this point something must be said of the framework, the milieu in which these events occurred, and something of the world as it existed at that time in terms of an Italian radical. I say an Italian radical, because this is an accurate description, philosophically, of both Sacco and Vanzetti, whether we refer to them as anarchists, as communists, or as socialists. In any case, they are radicals. At that time, in the spring of 1920, the life of a radical was a most uneasy life. Attorney General Palmer had undertaken proceedings for wholesale deportation of reds. Actions against radicals of foreign extraction were particularly savage, and very often these actions were taken in such terms as one finds difficult to accept today. For example, and pertinent to this inquiry, is the case of one Salsedo, an Italian, a radical, and a printer, who, in the spring of 1920, was held incommunicado in a room that was one of the offices of the Department of Justice—on the fourteenth floor of a building on Park Row in New York. The Italian Boda, who owned the car, and his comrades, were friends of the printer Salsedo. When they learned, on the fourth of May, that the smashed body of Salsedo had been found dead on the sidewalk outside of the building on Park Row, after having fallen by force or accident, fourteen stories, they felt that a threat against themselves was imminent. They had radical literature which they felt the necessity to hide. There were friends of theirs who they felt were in danger and must be notified. In order to do these things, Boda's car would be helpful, and Boda and three friends called to see if the car was ready. They were told that the car was not ready, and no sooner had they left than Mrs. Johnson, the wife of the man who owned the garage, notified the police.

"Sacco and Vanzetti were two of the men who had come to call for the car with Boda. After leaving the garage, Sacco and Vanzetti got on a street car. A police officer boarded the car with them, and arrested them on the car. They appeared to have no notion as to why they were arrested; they made no resistance; they went with him quietly and peaceably.

"There, in so many words, we have a picture of the situation which began a series of events which, lasting through seven years, have brought these two unfortunate men to where they are today.

"Until now, I have spoken of the crime. Even the simplest crime becomes exceedingly complex when approached legalistically. However, the question which I desire to deal with today, has less to do with the nature of the crime than the nature of the evidence. I am sure you have no-

54

ticed by now that the problem of evidence appears to be
a fairly simple one. It consists in the identification of
Nicola Sacco and Bartolomeo Vanzetti as two of the four-
man gang in the car, or on the street, when the payroll
was stolen and the murders were committed. But before
we get to details of evidence, it must be noted that at the
time of their arrest, Sacco and Vanzetti spoke English very
poorly. Neither of them, at the time, could make himself
clearly understood in the English language, nor was either
of them capable of comprehending the meaning of English
directed at him and spoken quickly. In the seven years
since then, this situation has changed, and as prisoners,
both of these men have applied themselves to the language and have, to a large extent, mastered it. However,
at that time, they often misunderstood questions put to
them, and answers which they gave were misinterpreted.
The court interpreter who was used, indulged in practices
which raise grave doubts as to his honesty. Sacco and Vanzetti were brought to trial more than a year after they were
arrested. The trial continued for seven weeks. On June 14,
1921, these two men were found guilty of murder in the
first degree.

"I said before that the main issue of evidence was the
identification of Sacco and Vanzetti as two of the murder
gang. During the course of the trial, fifty-nine witnesses
testified for the prosecution, for the Commonwealth of
Massachusetts. Their testimony included statements that
they had seen the defendants in South Braintree on the
morning of the murder, that they had recognized Sacco
as one of the murderers, and Vanzetti as one of the people
in the car. On the other hand, witnesses for the defense

55

provided both Sacco and Vanzetti with alibis. Sworn witnesses for the defense testified that on April 15, Sacco was in Boston, making inquiries concerning a passport to Italy. These witnesses are supported in their testimony by an official of the Italian consulate, who deposed that Sacco had visited the consulate in Boston at 2:15 p.m., the day that the murder took place. Witnesses for Vanzetti testified that on April 15, the day the murder took place, he was pursuing his trade as a fish peddler, a goodly distance from South Braintree, at the very time the murders were committed. In other words, witness after witness gave sworn testimony to the fact that it would have been utterly impossible for either Sacco or Vanzetti to have been involved in the crime which was committed at South Braintree.

"One would think, in the light of this, that questions of the guilt or innocence of Sacco and Vanzetti could not readily arise or find any support among thoughtful people. However, it is not quite so simple, nor are all people thoughtful in that sense. There were also numerous witnesses for the Commonwealth of Massachusetts, who swore under oath that Sacco and Vanzetti took part in the crime. Thus we are faced with the question of totally contradictory evidence.

"I will not and cannot, in the time I have here, go into a witness by witness examination of the evidence or of the character of those who gave evidence. I desire instead to establish some general conditions as to the trustworthiness of evidence funneled through the eyes of angry or prejudiced people. One witness, for example, gave a most extraordinary performance in powers of observation, memory and recollection. It is worth repeating here, because it is so typical of the manner in which these identifications of Sacco and Vanzetti as the criminals were obtained. This witness' name is Mary E. Splaine. Shortly after the crime was committed, the Pinkerton Detective Agency showed Miss Splaine some rogues' gallery pictures of criminals, and Miss Splaine selected a picture of one Tony Palmisano as a bandit she saw in the automobile. However, fourteen months later, she identified Nicola Sacco as the person seen in the automobile.

"The circumstances of her original observation of the crime are equally interesting. She was working on the second floor of a building across the street from where the murder occurred. When the explosion of shots sounded, she dropped her work and rushed to the window. You can imagine with what excitement such an action was accompanied. When she reached the window, the murder car was already pulling away, and thus, she had just a momentary glimpse of the car before it vanished. But fourteen months after she had that momentary glimpse, here is how she exercised her powers of recollection as a witness. I now quote from the trial record.

" 'Question: Can you describe him to these gentlemen here?'

"Whereupon, Miss Splaine answered: 'Yes, sir. He was a man that I should say was slightly taller than I am. He weighed possibly from 140 to 155 pounds. He was a muscular—he was an active looking man. I noticed particularly the left hand was a good-sized hand, a hand that denoted strength or a shoulder that—'

" 'Question: So that the hand you said you saw where?'

" 'Answer: The left hand, that was already on the back of the front seat, on the back of the front seat. He had a gray, what I thought was a shirt, had a grayish, like navy color, and the face was what we would call clear-cut, clean-cut face. Through here he was a little narrow, just a little narrow. The forehead was high. The hair was brushed back and it was between, I should think, two inches and two and one-half inches in length, and had dark eyebrows, but the complexion was a white, peculiar white that looked greenish.'

"'There is her description of what she had seen in that brief glimpse fourteen months before. Also, in the course of this recollection, she identified Nicola Sacco as the man she had seen. One would say, in the normal course of normal things, that such recollection under the circumstances, and such identification, is not only impossible, but to some extent, monstrous. Monstrous, that is, in a manner better explained through the experience of one Lewis Pelser. Like Miss Splaine, Pelser at first could not identify Sacco and Vanzetti, but again like Miss Splaine, he recovered remarkable powers of recall. At the time that Sacco and Vanzetti were arrested, Pelser was taken by the police to look at them. He stated that he could not possibly identify them as the criminals. Whereupon, Pelser, who worked for a shoe company closely associated with Slater and Morrill, the firm which had been robbed, was suddenly discharged and found himself jobless. A few weeks later, his power of recall freshened. He was re-employed by the same shoe company, and now he was suddenly able to identify Sacco and Vanzetti as the criminals. He was not the only one. In case after case, recollection and joblessness were intimately linked. Sometimes, when the weapon of discharge could not be employed, the District Attorney and those who cooperated with him on such matters, in their zealousness to bring the criminals to justice, used every manner of threat, both directly and by innuendo. Sometimes this procedure was so bare-faced that the proof of it remains for us in the trial record itself.

"It is indeed a bitter thing to have to give voice to accusations such as these, and enumerate conclusions such as I have enumerated, but they are to the point in the case of Sacco and Vanzetti. The execution scheduled for tonight is the logical outcome of that incredible and merciless trial. Certain people believe with great intensity that Sacco and Vanzetti cannot be allowed to remain alive. I state this gravely but unhesitatingly.

"It is important to recollect that the crime at South Braintree took place at a particular time, a strange, and to some extent, awful time in the history of this country. The passions of the entire country were inflamed by the notorious mass arrests which were instituted by Attorney General Palmer. Reds and Bolsheviks were everywhere, on every corner, in every dark alley, in every factory, and particularly in those factories where workers murmured that their wages were insufficient to feed and clothe their families. Strangely, or not so strangely, this condition created bewhiskered devils who, loaded with bombs, were found behind every bush—and the identity of these Bolsheviks and agitators with Americans of foreign extraction was implied if not stated every day in almost every newspaper in the land. Millions and millions of people were led to believe that there was a radical threat to the very existence of this country as a free nation. Within this inflamed situation, a particularly cold-blooded and brutal crime took place here in Massachusetts, and the fairly trustworthy identification of the criminals as Italians, further inflamed already existing prejudices. As the accused, Sacco and Vanzetti are brought into a courtroom. They are unable to speak English. They are frightened, harassed, poorly clothed, unkempt. Witness after witness is called to the stand and asked whether these two are, or resemble, the people who took part in the crime more than a year ago, so quickly committed and so violent in its reactions on people and impressions left upon memory. Witness after witness identifies Sacco and Vanzetti.

"Gentlemen, what, precisely, does this mean in terms of legal evidence? It is a part of what so many of us proudly refer to as Anglo-Saxon law, that a man is not to be convicted of murder, with his life in jeopardy, unless there is indisputable eye-witness evidence. Even though people have been convicted on circumstantial evidence, the fact remains, and the gravity, the profound gravity involved in the legal taking of human life, demands such precautions. Sacco and Vanzetti were convicted through eye-witness evidence. The rub is, gentlemen, that it was impossible for the eye-witness to be telling the truth; that far more trustworthy eye-witness evidence proves that Sacco and Vanzetti were miles from the scene of the crime when it was committed, and that one piece of circumstantial evidence remains quite unshakable.

"I come to that circumstantial evidence now. When Sacco and Vanzetti were arrested, Sacco possessed a pistol.

That pistol was introduced as evidence in the trial, and a famous ballistics expert, Captain Proctor by name, was called in to examine the pistol found on Sacco, and to offer an opinion as to whether a bullet taken from a murder victim's body was actually fired from this pistol. A capable ballistics expert is able to make a fairly certain determination in such cases, and Captain Proctor was considered to be this type of expert. He made his examination, and he came to the conclusion that the bullet used in the murder could not have been fired from the pistol owned by and found on Nicola Sacco. However, the District Attorney in the case seems to have discussed the matter with Captain Proctor, and rather than have his case shattered, prevailed upon Captain Proctor to answer the question: 'Have you an opinion as to whether bullet number three was fired from the Colt automatic which is in evidence [Sacco's pistol]?' in this strange manner: 'My opinion is that it is consistent with being fired from that pistol.'

"There is an answer, gentlemen, that will echo and re-echo for a long time in the pages of history. What does *consistent* mean in this case? The jury evidently took it to mean that he identified Sacco's pistol as the murder weapon. Such it would seem to me in plain English, as we know plain English. However, it meant nothing of the sort. It was the compromise decided upon by the District Attorney and the ballistics expert, and afterwards, in a deposition, this same ballistics expert said the following:

" 'Had I been asked the direct question: whether I had found any affirmative evidence whatever that this so-called mortal bullet had passed through this particular Sacco's pistol, I should have answered then, as I do now without hesitation, in the negative.'

"One would think, gentlemen, that this evidence, reversing the earlier statement of the ballistics expert and coming to light through a deposition filed in one of the appeals of Sacco and Vanzetti, would warrant a new trial. But that is not the case. I spoke of evidence before, as offered by people who see a thing with their own eyes. I have now balanced evidence against possibility, probability and certainty, because all too often one sees with one's eyes what one desires to see with one's eyes, even as a weak man says with his tongue, words which a venal district attorney and a prejudiced judge desire him to say. In the United States, in Massachusetts, and in South Braintree as well, a situation was created in 1920, which caused a number of people to desire to see men like Sacco and Vanzetti the accused and convicted in a murder case, and thereby as men deserving the death sentence. Were not these two men reds, and therefore enemies of all that is decent? Were they not radicals, and therefore unlike ordinary decent and upstanding citizens? Were they not against capitalism, which is certainly the only and God-given way of life in these United States? Were they not opposed to war, and had we not just finished a war to make the world safe for democracy—a war to which no decent and upright citizen could be opposed? Did they not speak sneeringly of the profit system, and were we not dedicated by God and the Constitution to an eternal system of industry which bases itself upon profits, upon the unflagging desire of one man to make more money than the

62

next, even if he has to sweat it out of his neighbor's hide?

"These, perhaps, are very harsh questions for me to ask, gentlemen, but I ask them so that you may be the better instructed in the practice of law. I know full well the gravity of my statements. But no man faces life until he reconciles his own actions with the situations imposed by life. This makes for gravity. It made for gravity in the case of Sacco and Vanzetti, and before today is over, they will be made to pay with their lives for the beliefs they held, not for the crimes they committed. Evidence, gentlemen, can be master or servant, as I have shown to some degree, and will show even more concretely. . . ."

The professor lectured for twenty minutes more, yet when he had finished, he sensed that a very important thing he had wanted to say, remained unsaid. He had wanted to say that in a court ruled, owned and operated by the University President, the Governor of the Commonwealth and the Judge who sat in judgment, there could be no justice for two men like Sacco and Vanzetti. Yet if he had said just that, he would have closed all doors to his own future.

The lecture was over, but still he was held rigid by his thoughts. He felt a peculiar and particular weakness that always came upon him after he had been lecturing for a long while, and he wished, as always, that he could be immediately alone; but the students crowded around him, and some of them thanked him, and others clung stubbornly to things he had said. One of them expressed it thus,

"But surely, sir, they will not execute them tonight. What can we do? There must be something that we can do."

"I am afraid there is nothing we can do," he answered.

"But you don't mean to infer, sir, that all of law is a mockery, that courts are worthless, and that there is no justice?"

This shocked him. He stared at the student who had challenged him with this, a red-headed, bright-eyed lad, and suddenly the Professor became even more somber, sober, and afraid. Well, it was a time for being afraid, the Professor thought ruefully.

"Did you mean that, sir?" the student insisted.

"If I meant that," he found himself saying, "then my own life would be as wasted as yours."

"Yet, everything you say adds up to injustice. How can there be justice if all forces of law create injustice?"

"Well, of course, that would be another lecture, wouldn't it?"

He looked at his watch. He made excuses, and rushed away, shaking off the reporters who plucked at his sweat-soaked clothes and threw their eager questions after him.

Chapter 5

FINISHED with his breakfast and half way through his second cup of coffee, the President of the University stared fixedly at the portrait of Ralph Waldo Emerson, narrowed his eyes, and belched. He belched with prerogative, if not with grace; he picked his nose in the same way; this was what someone in the English department had referred to as "the lordly simplicity of arrogance," partly an aphorism, and in part a non sequitur. He did things that would have marked another of like venerability as a dirty old man, but his fierce and somewhat incredible snobbishness still exempted him from that designation.

The instructor sitting opposite him finished his tale.

"Only now, only five minutes ago," the University President said with disbelief. "It passes one's understanding. I tell you, the Jew has erupted like a volcano. We will never hear the end of him." Once again, he fixed his eyes—which someone had described as piercing—upon the portrait of Emerson. "I speak not of one man, but in general terms, when I say *the Jew*," he explained. "Would you repeat what he said—the part about a thirst for blood?"

"I wouldn't say he used just those words—"

At that moment the Dean of the Law School entered. He sniffed wrath, and joined himself to it. He assumed a station at one side of the broad, pleasant dining room, with its fine Chippendale furniture, its hand-blocked wall paper, and its lovely and faded eighteenth century hooked rug, placing himself directly under the portrait of Henry Thoreau, his hands folded comfortably across his plump, protruding belly.

"He is on his way up here, sir," he said, trying to combine in one smirk both regret and anticipation. The President, however, paid no mind whatsoever to him, driving hard on the young instructor.

"No—no indeed? But so you reported it."

"In effect, sir. I wish to be scrupulous."

"A commendable desire not shared by too many," said the President of the University.

"In my desire to be scrupulous, I must of necessity report his words with some scrupulousness. He inferred that there were certain people in high places who, out of a taste for blood also inferred, desired with absoluteness the death of these two Italians, Sacco and Vanzetti."

"Ha! Precisely! A taste for blood."

"Implicit, sir, if I may."

"Did you hear?" he asked the Dean of the Law School. The Dean nodded. "Not stated, but implied."

"And you did not stop him?"

"I hardly could," the Dean of the Law School protested.

"I came into the room after he had been speaking for at least fifteen minutes, and I felt, quite correctly, I think, that any attempt to halt him would have been far more disastrous than anything he might say. This is something for us to consider, for he has placed himself in a powerful position, if I may say so. He is shrewd. He shares that quality."

"With his race. They live on shrewdness. But I don't see his position as so powerful. He has slandered honest men, and he must be made to pay for that. I am an old man, sir."

"Many younger men have less vigor and youth."

"That may be. Nevertheless, I must husband myself. The strength I use cannot be replaced. When a man passes seventy years, death sits at his elbow. Nevertheless, I did not spare myself. When I was called upon for public service, I came forward. I did not say that these were Italians. Am I prejudiced against Latins? Some would say I am prejudiced against Jews. Not so. Not so!" he repeated. "My ancestors planted a sturdy race on this soil, clear-eyed and fair of feature. We dealt with no such names as Sacco and Vanzetti then, but of Lodges and Cabots and Bruces and Winthrops and Butlers and Proctors and Emersons, there were plenty indeed. And when I look around me to-day—where is that race? Yet I did not use this when I was called upon. When the head of this ancient Common-wealth asked me to serve in inquiry, weighing the facts in this case that has made our land like a trollop's name on the lips of people everywhere, I did not refuse. I served. I examined the facts. I sorted the wheat from the chaff. I—"

He was interrupted in his words by the entrance of the Professor of Criminal Law; and then at that moment it seemed to the two men in attendance, the Dean of the Law School and the instructor, that the Professor of Criminal Law walked, indeed, where wiser men—and even angels—would fear to tread. Uncomely, squinting behind his glasses, he lumbered into the room and faced the President of the University.

"You wanted to see me?" he asked bluntly.

The President found he was trembling a little. "Age," he thought to himself. "I am not properly armed for anger." And he said deliberately, "I heard that at your lecture this morning, you said some things that a thoughtful man might find reason to regret."

"The reports came quickly," answered the Professor calmly, "but I said nothing that I see reason to regret. Nor do I consider myself unusually thoughtless."

"Consider again, sir!"

"I have considered well and seriously," the Professor replied. "I have lost count of the hours I spent weighing these matters. I decided that what must be said, must be said."

For all the care with which he spoke, there was more than a trace of a foreign accent in the voice of the Professor. Some of his formulations carried that awkwardness which suggested echoes of another tongue, and when he pronounced a word ending with *ing*, he could not prevent the *k* sound from creeping in. Of these things, the President of the University was acutely aware; but his awareness was brushed all over with irritation, and this made him

68

even more irascible than he ordinarily was. For several days now, he had contained within himself a fine comfortable feeling of achievement and power at the decision he and his companions on the investigating committee had come to. Never, never would he put it so bluntly and vulgarly as the Judge in the case had put it, when the Judge said, *Well, I did give those anarchist bastards what was coming to them!* Yet he couldn't deny that he felt something of the same thing that the Judge must have felt. But all morning now, that feeling of achievement had been slipping away, dissipating, and when he heard of the ill-considered—as he thought of it—and violent lecture the Professor had given, the remainder of that feeling of achievement quickly disappeared.

What did they mean, he wondered now, when they said that the Professor was in a powerful position? Did they mean that approval—approval of decent people, and some not too unlike himself, old people well-located in Boston—might rest with the Professor of Criminal Law? Could they mean such a thing?

"You are very sure of yourself, sir," the President said coldly.

"Yes—yes, I think I am."

"And that gave you the right and the purpose to accuse people of desiring the death of these two men?"

"People do desire it—a few people in high places. The world knows it. I said it. I don't regret saying it."

"Meaning myself?"

"Sir?"

"You accuse me?"

"No—I never mentioned you," the Professor said. "*You* accuse *yourself*, sir. Your feelings are hurt, but these two men will die tonight. How many times have you died, sir?"

"You are being insufferable!"

"Am I? Was their lawyer also insufferable? He was more eloquent than I am. I read his argument only once, but it remained with me. How did he conclude—*if you cannot give these men a fair trial, pardon them, pardon them by all that is holy. Christians created a God that is merciful. You sit like God, with life in your hand.* Did he say that or something like that? Only yesterday. Shall I forget that you enjoyed being executioner?"

Anger went away, and suddenly the President of the University was afraid. His ancestors were a poor, cold shroud. His ears hummed, as if that man the Professor of Criminal Law had just referred to, the lawyer of Sacco and Vanzetti, were standing before him again.

"Sit down," he had said then to that other lawyer who had appeared before him a few days ago to make a last plea—standing before him then even as this Jew stood before him now. "Why must you stand and pace like that?" "I cannot argue sitting," the lawyer had answered. "I cannot plead sitting. I am pleading now. If you cannot give these men a new trial, having heard so much evidence, then they should be pardoned. They are not to blame if the State of Massachusetts employs a judge who refers to men on trial before him as 'anarchistic bastards,' tells about how he will get them, and that 'that will hold them,' and boasts about what he had done to them and what he is going to do. Sacco and Vanzetti did not appoint him and are not to blame if the State of Massachusetts tolerates him.

70

"If the Supreme Court of this State has no jurisdiction to alter what a judge has said, because it has to protect the discretion vested in the judge, then the only thing the State can do is to pardon these men, humiliating as it may be, humiliating as it is to every citizen in this State to have to admit that men can be treated as these men have been treated. We have to stomach it, to stand it; there is no way out of it. And any attempt to evade this, to gloss it over, to make black white, to stamp it down, to suppress it, will not do any good. Everybody is familiar with the case, all over the world. This evidence has been translated into every European language. They are as familiar with it in Germany and France as we are. We are up against the wall.

"The ablest men in Massachusetts who respect the courts are forced into a corner. We have got either to make some explanation that won't be accepted and that really can't commend itself to our own judgment as sincere, candid and fair, or else we have got to admit that this trial was a mistake and a miscarriage of justice, that it was unfairly conducted, that there was a reasonable doubt, which has been enormously increased since, and that our courts have been unable to correct the error then made, and therefore the Governor should pardon these men, whether or not you now believe they are guilty, whether or not you think that in five years from now the evidence would be stronger against them or weaker against them. The day has gone by, the State has had its chance, the trial has occurred. These arguments have all taken place. The courts have finished, and this is the result of this case.

"Now I am through with this case. I have done the best

I could with it. I have labored here for years trying to bring about elementary justice, and if I fail I shall feel bitterly disappointed but not remorseful. I have done what I could, and I ask you to do what you can to prevent what, if not prevented, will be to the everlasting disgrace of this State."

"Sit down, can't you?" was all he could think of saying to the lawyer then—when that argument was made. He had not even heard, with any perception, the words he remembered so cruelly now. But, finished with his plea, the lawyer for Sacco and Vanzetti had remained standing and looking at him, even as the Professor of Criminal Law now looked at him; and in his mind, the University President tried to formulate words that would not take shape. Words like *I shall have to ask for your resignation.* But he did not and could not speak those words. "All alone," he said to himself.

"You're an old man," the Professor of Criminal Law said bitterly, "and yet you love death. Old man, you're an executioner!"

"How dare you talk like that!"

The instructor watched and listened in horrified silence, but the Dean of the Law School cried, "Have you lost your mind?"

"Oh, no—no, not at all. Why am I wanted here?"

The old man, who was one of the high aristocrats of a nation that supposedly had no aristocracy, suddenly re-read once again the document he had signed, and signed it again in his mind's eye, his old hand trembling, as his eyes traveled down the lines he himself had dictated:

"The alibi of Vanzetti is decidedly weak. One of the witnesses, Rosen, seems to the Committee to have been shown by the cross-examination to have been lying at the trial; another, Mrs. Brini, had sworn to an alibi for him in the Bridgewater case, and two more of the witnesses did not seem certain of the date until they had talked it over. Under these circumstances, if he was with Sacco, or in the bandits' car, or indeed in South Braintree at all that day, he was undoubtedly guilty; for there is no reason why, if he was there for an innocent purpose, he should have sworn that he was in Plymouth all day. Now there are four persons who testified that they had seen him;—Dolbeare, who says he saw him in the morning in a car on the main street of South Braintree; Levangie, who said he saw him—erroneously at the wheel—as the car crossed the tracks after the shooting; and Austin T. Reed, who says that Vanzetti swore at him from the car at the Matfield railroad crossing. The fourth man was Faulkner, who testified that he was asked a question by Vanzetti in a smoking car on the way from Plymouth to South Braintree on the forenoon of the day of the murder, and that he saw him alight at that station. Faulkner's testimony is impeached on two grounds: First that he said the car was a combination smoker and baggage car, and that there was no such car on that train, but his description of the interior is exactly that of a full smoking car; and second, that no ticket that could be so used was sold that morning at any of the stations in or near Plymouth, and that no such cash fare was paid or mileage book punched, but that does not exhaust the possibilities. Otherwise no one claims to have seen him, or any man resembling him who was not Vanzetti. But it must be remembered that his face is much more unusual, and more

73

easily remembered, than that of Sacco. He was evidently not in the foreground. On the whole, we are of the opinion that Vanzetti also was guilty beyond reasonable doubt.

"It has been urged that a crime of this kind must have been committed by professionals, and it is for well-known criminal gangs that one must look; but to the Committee, both this crime and the one at Bridgewater do not seem to bear the marks of professionals, but of men inexpert in such crimes."

Such was the President's summation, after his Committee had heard the evidence. This he had signed—just as one signs a death warrant. Why was he afraid now, when he had played the executioner then with such certainty?

"Why am I wanted here?" the Professor of Criminal Law repeated. "To be scolded? To be asked for a resignation? I will not resign. To be Jew-baited? I will not be Jew-baited."

"You are insufferable, sir. Get out of here!" the President of the University cried.

"You are an old man, but Sacco is only thirty-six years old, and Vanzetti is not yet forty. There is death all over you, old man, death and hatred." And with that, the Professor of Criminal Law turned on his heel and walked out.

Behind him, he left a room fixed and riveted in silence and with no motion except the trembling of the old man who had name and wealth and honor and position and was now as bankrupt as a man could be, frightened and heavily aware of death. But for the Professor of Criminal Law, there was no victory either. He had been able to say

what he pleased because his position was strong; he was
wrapped in a mantle of righteousness; but how much had
he himself left undone and unsaid? Did he even understand with any sort of clarity why these two must die? Or
was that something he was afraid to challenge with understanding?

Chapter 6

AT ELEVEN O'CLOCK, reinforcements came rolling up to Charlestown Prison, and people who saw this had the impression that a small war had begun and these troops were hurtling out to meet the enemy. There were armed men sitting in cars, motorcycles with tommy gunners in the side cars, and a searchlight truck able to produce a beam that could cut through fog and nightfall for fully three miles. With sirens screaming, this cavalcade rolled up and halted before the prison; and the Warden, who had been told earlier that trouble might be expected and that reinforcements were on their way, went out to greet them, and eyed them most dubiously.

When the chief of the state police had first called the Warden and said that, acting upon instructions of the Governor, he was sending additional forces to the prison, the Warden replied querulously and with a good deal of annoyance.

"What kind of trouble?" the Warden wanted to know.

They did not say what kind of trouble. They had no way of knowing what kind of trouble. It just seemed that there was trouble in the making, and that they ought to be prepared to meet it.

"Well, if you feel that way about it, I suppose that's your feeling and you have got some basis for it," the Warden said to the chief of police, thinking to himself that there was plenty of trouble and would be a good deal more before this bitter day finished; but not that kind of trouble. What did they think, the Warden wondered? Did they think that an army was coming to blast through the prison walls and take out the two anarchists? In his own thoughts, the Warden was somewhat defensive about Sacco and Vanzetti. He had come to believe that he was possessed of an area of knowledge about the condemned men denied to the average man and woman; and he knew very well what mild and quiet people these poor devils were. That was such knowledge as grew inside of a prison and nowhere else. The Warden could think back to many years of learning how mild and quiet some people were, people whom the whole outside world condemned with one voice.

Now he went outside to talk to the captain of the state police, who headed up the semi-military detachment; and the Warden told him sourly that he could use his own judgment in stationing his men here and there—wherever he saw fit.

"What kind of trouble do you expect?" the captain of the state police asked him.

"I don't expect trouble," the Warden snapped. "Not your kind of trouble, anyway."

Then he went back to his office, leaving the captain of police to say to a lieutenant, "Now what in hell is eating him? You'd just think he had some call to take our heads off!"

The Warden returned to his office, his face as dark and threatening as a cloud-filled sky. Several people who were waiting outside of his office and had one thing and another to discuss with him, changed their minds and decided that what they had to talk about would hold until his mood changed a little; that is, all except the electrician, for like the Warden, the electrician had not chosen this day but had instead been confronted with it, and he had things to discuss with the Warden whether the Warden's face was solemn or not. He entered the Warden's office and pointed out to him with necessary bluntness that here it was a quarter of an hour past eleven o'clock in the morning, and he had not tested the current.

"Well, why the devil don't you test it?" the Warden wanted to know.

"Only because I was told to see you and talk to you before I tested it," the electrician answered defensively.

The Warden now remembered that he had given those instructions. It was just a small kindness he had thought of, for it did no good for the prison population to see the lights wax and wane, grow dim, and then come on again. When that happened, they knew everywhere in the prison that juice was being fed into the electric chair, and that here was a sort of rehearsal for the taking of life. Not being a completely insensitive man, the Warden was aware that every prisoner in the place shared to some extent in the suffering of the three doomed men, and waited for the time of execution with fear and at least some heartsickness. The prison bound its population into a unit that was like

78

a living body, and when a part of this body died, a little of each individual also died. People who have never been in prison, worked in a prison, or done time in a prison, might be at a loss to understand just how this is, or even unwilling to believe that plain, ordinary criminals could feel such sympathy with men who are condemned to death. Nevertheless, the Warden knew this unity of pain to be a fact. He did not like to prod such feelings on the part of hundreds of men needlessly, and he was also capable of picturing the specific kind of mental pain the little dress rehearsal with electric current would bring to Sacco and Vanzetti and Madeiros. While they had to die many times before this day was finished, do what anyone might, it seemed needlessly cruel to inject this added bit of horror.

The Warden said some of this to the electrician, who agreed, but pointed out that there was nothing he could do about it.

"The way it is," the electrician said, "you can never be sure that your wiring or your fuses are going to stand up under the load that you have to feed into that chair. Just between you and me, sir, that's the God-damnedest way to kill a human being that anybody ever thought of, and why they ever thought of it beats the hell out of me. It just doesn't make no sense at all to put a man into an electric chair and send current into his body. If they think it is painless, then they are crazy. You just have to see it happen once to know how painless it is! I tell you this—if I had the choice myself between this kind of thing and being hanged, I'd want to be hanged. I'd want to be shot, or anything rather than to have to sit down in that chair."

"I'm not asking about your feelings on the subject, mister," the Warden said testily. "All I ask is why you have to test that damn chair all day long?"

"Just for this reason," the electrician explained. "Suppose you put one of them into it and throw the current and it shorts. Let's say a wire burns out or a fuse goes. Well, that's a pretty situation, isn't it? That would make a fine situation, to have one of them poor devils sitting there with the electrodes on and with his eyes bandaged, and then to have to wait two hours before the break could be re-wired, or the short found, and then the execution could go on again."

"Well, we don't want that to happen," the Warden said. "You can be sure that's the last thing in the world I want to happen. But why can't you test it once this evening?"

"It just doesn't work that way," the electrician explained. "You have to keep testing it and finding the weak spots. You build up the weak spots so that when the night time comes, there are no weak spots left, and you know that when you throw juice in, it's going to hold up under it, and so is the regular prison lighting system going to hold up."

"All right, then. The hell with it," the Warden said. "Go on and do whatever you have to do."

The electrician nodded and left the Warden's office, and a little while later, sitting in their cells, Sacco and Van-zetti saw the lights dim, remain dim for a moment or two, and then grow strong again. Each of them became rigid when this happened. In more than a manner of speaking, they died while they lived.

There were only three cells in the Death Row in the State Prison. The builders of this particular wing of the prison—which was known as Cherry Hill, for some strange reason—had not pictured a contingency where there would ever be more than three men awaiting execution at one time. Therefore, Death Row consisted of three cheerless, airless, and lightless cells. They were all in one row, side by side, and instead of the customary barred door that most prison cells have, these three cells had heavy wooden doors with only a small grill in each door. Therefore, it was necessary to light these cells artificially; and to people inside, the cells seemed to shrink, to dwindle, to fold in upon themselves with particularized intensity and exceedingly slow horror, when the wiring system of the prison was tested.

As Nicola Sacco sat upon the edge of his cot and watched this happen, he heard a violent cry, sharp and piercing and loaded with sudden, unbearable pain, as an animal's cry might be; and it came from the cell next door, Madeiros' cell. This cry died away and was then followed by a series of moans; and in all his life, Sacco felt, he had never heard anything so pitiful, so utterly wretched and bereft as these moans of the poor, damned and frightened thief. Then, with ears acutely accustomed to every change of sound, he heard Madeiros fall prone upon his cot and begin to weep. This was more than Sacco could bear. He leaped up, ran to the door of his cell, and shouted through the opening,

"Madeiros, Madeiros, do you hear me?"

"I hear you. What do you want?" Madeiros asked through his tears.

"I want to comfort you a little. I want you to take heart."

Even as he said this, Sacco wondered what on earth

there was to comfort any one of the three of them, and from where indeed they could take heart or hope? As an echo of his own thoughts, Madeiros answered,

"What's there to take heart in?"

"There's still hope."

"For you, maybe, Mr. Sacco. Maybe there is still hope for you, but there is no hope for me. I am going to die. Nothing in the whole world can change that. In just a little while, I am going to die."

"Now isn't that nonsense!" Sacco cried, feeling better now that he had to struggle with the fears of another. "That's real nonsense, Madeiros. They can't take your life until they take ours. So long as they keep us alive, they must keep you alive too, for you are the most important material witness to the whole affair of Sacco and Vanzetti. Now look—just you look at it this way. Why do you think the three of us are here together? We are here together because our fortunes are linked. There is nothing to cry about yet."

"Isn't death something to cry about?" Madeiros asked woefully, as a child might ask a totally pathetic and obvious question—the answer to which was equally pathetic and obvious.

"You keep saying death. Now is no time to think of death and talk about death, just because they want to play with their lights. Well, who cares about that? Who cares what they do with their lights? Let them turn the lights on and off all day long if that's the way they feel about it!"

"They are testing the electric chair in which we are going to die."

"Oh, there you go again!" cried Sacco. "Nothing but death! The trouble is, you have given up."

"That's right. I have given up. It's all wasted."

"What is wasted?"

"My whole life is wasted. Nothing ever came of it. It was wrong. From the first day I was born, it was wrong and wasted. But I never made it that way. Do you understand, Mr. Sacco? I never made it that way. Something else made it that way. I spoke to Mr. Vanzetti about it once, and he tried to explain to me some of the things that made it that way. I listened very carefully while he explained it. I would begin to understand something he says and then I don't understand it any more. You know what I am talking about, Mr. Sacco?"

"I know," Sacco said. "Poor boy—of course I know."

"But it was all wasted."

Sacco said, "Life is never wasted. Madeiros, I swear to you that I am telling you a most profound truth. Life is never wasted. It is wrong for you now to think that your whole life was wasted just because you did some things that might have been bad. How was it with my own sweet little boy? If he did bad things, did I lock him up in a dark room? No. I tried to explain to him. I tried to show him that there are good ways and that there are bad ways. Sometimes it was very hard to make him see the difference, because a little boy is not a fully grown and wise man. Well, that was because he had a father; he was lucky to have a father to explain things. But when someone does something when they are eighteen or nineteen or twenty years old, the way you did, Madeiros, well, then it is something else. Nobody bothers to take a little time and sit down with you and try to make it clear and plain what is a good thing and what is a bad thing."

He heard Madeiros start to weep again, and he shouted to him, "Madeiros, Madeiros, please, I did not want to say anything to make you more sorrowful. I was only trying to explain to you that life is not wasted. I think of it this way—you want me to tell you how I think of it, Madeiros?"

"Yes, tell me, Mr. Sacco, please," the thief said. "I am sorry if I cry. That is because sometimes things happen to me that I can't control. I don't want to have a fit, but then sometimes I have a fit. I don't want to cry, but then I just go and cry, whether I want to or not."

"I understand how that is," Sacco answered gently. "Now here is what I meant, Madeiros. I meant that every human life in the whole world is connected with every other human life. It is just like there were threads that you can't see from every one of us to every other one of us. In the worst terrible moments, when I am filled with such hatred for the judge who is so cruel and so unfeeling in the way he sentenced us, I still say to myself, he must not be hated unreasonably. He is a part of human beings the way you are. He too is connected with little threads to all of us. Only he has become filled with sickness and hatred. Do you see what I mean, Madeiros?"

"I am trying all I can to understand," Madeiros answered. "It is not your fault if I don't understand."

"But life is not wasted," Sacco insisted. He raised his voice and called to Vanzetti for confirmation. "Bartolomeo! Bartolomeo!" he called. "Have you been listening?"

"I have been listening," Vanzetti said, standing up against

84

the door of his own cell, the tears running softly and effortlessly down his face.

"And am I not right when I tell Madeiros here that no human life is ever wasted?"

"You are right," Vanzetti answered. "Nick, you are very right, and filled with wisdom. Listen to him when he says something, Madeiros. He is very wise and kind."

At that moment the prison bells began to ring, clanging out the noonday hour. It was now twelve o'clock, high noon, on August 22, 1927.

Chapter 7

HIGH NOON in the city of Boston and the Commonwealth of Massachusetts is six hours away, measuring distance with zones of time, from Rome in Italy. When it is twelve o'clock on the Eastern Seaboard of the United States, the late afternoon shadows are already settling over the beautiful antique ruins, the lovely open squares, and the hot and miserable slums of Rome.

It was the time when the Dictator took his afternoon exercise before he dressed for dinner. Today he sparred with light gloves. The exercise was not absolutely routine, nor always the same, for on some days he skipped rope; on other days he boxed; and again, he would fence with the ancient Roman shield and shortsword. He prided himself on his physical prowess; and when he sparred in what he liked to refer to as "the American manner," he drove in close, giving his opponent no quarter and showing no mercy. Whether with good or bad grace, the unfortunate sparring partner had to take the punishment, realizing that there were natural limits to the sense of sportsmanship shown even by this most sportsman-like of rulers. On the other hand, the Dictator enjoyed the bodily contact of boxing, the solid smack of leather against flesh, and the feeling of physical conquest and achievement that came from it.

A fine and healthy routine consisted of ten minutes of furious peddling upon the stationary bicycle; five minutes of rowing in the stationary shell; ten minutes of sparring with two sparring partners—the two sparring partners being a special sop to the Dictator's conceit—a plunge, and then a stinging, refreshing, ice cold needle shower.

Naked as the day he was born, the Dictator would prance out of his shower, slapping his chest and inhaling mighty breaths of air, while three attendants rubbed his skin and toweled him. He loved to do this in front of a mirror, so that he could enjoy watching his own chest expansion and take pleasure in his robust limbs and his healthy, clear skin. Very often he would follow this with a massage. He enjoyed the sensual pleasure of stretching out on the rubbing table while the expert fingers of the masseur explored every muscle and tendon in his body; and at such moments he felt a certain excitement in his very nakedness, giving himself completely and dangerously to the mercy of the masseur. Naked and unprotected, he lay there, loose and relaxed, while the blood began to course speedily and freely through his limbs and his skin tingled with new life.

Such moments were highly sensual, and very often he occupied them in planning some small pleasure he might grant himself in the hour that remained before his dinner time. He needed to deny himself no such pleasures, and he was fond of saying to his intimates that no passage with a woman was as rewarding or as delightful as that which occurred in the afternoon, before one's evening meal. Today he played with this thought, and created images in those special recesses of his mind reserved for and devoted to this game. He allowed a full massage today. He stretched like a great cat while the oil was poured on him and all the kinks and tensions of the day were rubbed out of his limbs. It was most fitting that he should plan both love and amusement, as well as certain significant matters of state, while this was going on; and when he stood on his feet again, he was stimulated not only by the physical massage, but by the excitement of his thoughts as well. He examined himself with new interest in the mirror. He peered at the flesh over his abdomen, and tested it for any softness or bulk that might indicate approaching middle age.

Age terrified him, even as death terrified him, and his worst moments came when he reflected upon age or death. Recently he had been thinking of both of these unhappy states a little more than the circumstances of his life and position seemed to warrant.

The circumstances in themselves were quite good, for never—it seemed to him—had his own position or the position of the country been better. The last pockets of resistance in the land had been eliminated. The menace of communism had been crushed decisively—and once and forever; and only a few days before, he had stood proudly and fiercely upon his balcony, facing a great sea of human faces, hundreds and thousands of people pressed together, who roared in unison the thunderous ovation of,

"Duce! Duce! Duce!"

He spoke of what he had achieved for them. He informed them that the Bolshevik menace, the Godless, fanged monster of communism, had been slain, even as once so long ago, the dragons of perfidy had been slain by the champions of chivalry. Italian Bolshevism was dead; Italian communism was dead. There was order all over the land, and for fascism, a thousand fruitful years; during which years the riches of the whole world would reward those who believed, obeyed, and followed.

In spite of this, in spite of the great ovation he had received, in spite of the adulation of everyone around him, in spite of the increased respect he was winning on the diplomatic front from the great nations he so envied and admired— France, Britain and the United States of America—in spite of the proof that his physical prowess was undiminished and his ability to play the part of a noble stallion in no way impaired—in spite of all these happy circumstances, he had been unduly depressed of late, and more than a little worried and perturbed that he could not locate the source of his depression.

Only a few nights ago, he had dined with a well known Viennese psychiatrist—he had a compelling if secret admiration for the profession—and had placed before this psychiatrist the question of whether or not he, the psychiatrist, believed that the ancient Roman emperors were convinced of their own godliness and their own immortality?

"Well, sir," the Viennese had replied," you must take those two things separately. Godliness and immortality are not synonymous. It is only today that we reward the gods with eternal life. In ancient times, there were gods who lived for exceedingly long periods, and there were others who perished even as men perish. But it is questionable whether the ancient civilizations even conceived of the gods as immortal; they had really never posed this particular problem for themselves, since they were not troubled, as we are, by a hunger for eternal life.

The Dictator wondered whether this was actually the case. Not infrequently, the Dictator identified himself with the ancient rulers of Imperial Rome. A Tuscan sculptors' guild had made him a gift of three busts of Romans of long ago who resembled him so greatly that they might each of them have been his twin. Also, it was not uncommon for him to dream that he was a god, and then in the first hours of waking from such a dream, be unable to separate the god from himself or himself from the god. He would laugh at himself rather easily and good naturedly for indulging his own small fancies, but at the same time he would reserve to himself the conviction that many great mysteries remained unknown to and unsolved by either science or philosophy. Very lightly, with surprising humor, he conveyed this to the Austrian psychiatrist; for he knew that all men talked, and particularly that they liked to gossip about the great, and he had no desire to have it voiced around that he cherished such illusions of himself as intimations of godliness. The Austrian psychiatrist, however, being sensitive to the slightest wish of the Dictator, sensed what was in the Dictator's mind, and pursued the question himself, making it plain to the Dictator that he, the Dictator, had as much right to godliness as any successor of Julius Caesar.

"We know so little about the body," the psychiatrist said reasonably. "Its mysteries are endless and almost untouched. Consider the ductless glands—what secrets they might reveal if they were ever made to talk to us in their own language of chemistry, is almost beyond man's imagination. Who is to say that man is dust?—out of dust and into dust again? Why do men die? We can only guess. Old age itself is a mystery."

"But all men do die," the Dictator argued, pressing the point so that the psychiatrist might lead the conversation further on the same road.

"Do they?" The Viennese raised his brow. "How do we know? Have we a record of the births and deaths of all men? Consider this, sir. Suppose that a man's body and spirit conquered mortality, not mystically, but with its own inner chemistry? He would find that as the years passed, he grew no older; and once the suggestion of such evidence became an actual fact, he would have to meet the situation and cope with it. In other words, though he lived, he would have to simulate death, he would have to disappear, he would have to concoct a suicide, he would have to emigrate, flee, move from city to city. How do we know that this has not been the case with many people? If it were the case, such secrets would be the most carefully kept secrets that any human being could own; for if it were known by the lesser breed who must of a certainty die when their mortal time comes, then they would turn upon the immortal and destroy him as mercilessly as wolves drag down a deer."

The Dictator hung on every word of this fantastic peroration, and while he tried to mask the eagerness and rapt attention with which he listened, his powers of concealment were less than suited to this particular need.

"But if such a gift were granted to men of power, they would not have to hide and skulk."

"But how many men of power have there been since history began?" the psychiatrist asked softly. "If we look upon this thing statistically, then we must grant that there have been too few men of power to test it—real power, I mean—the indisputable power that once in a millenium is vested in one man of immense strength, wisdom, conviction and control. . . ."

That conversation had been one of the most truly rewarding and wonderful things the Dictator had ever experienced. And the night it took place, he slept like a baby, without fear or presentiment of evil—nor did he face any of the cold mental horrors of his own death without resurrection in the lonely moments before he slept.

Today, however, coming out of what should have been the totally satisfying stimulation and relaxation of exercise, bath and massage, he felt gloomy and ill at ease; and he wondered why his peace of mind had fled so suddenly. He was wrapping himself in a great towel-robe, preparatory to going to his dressing room, when his secretary came in with a handful of notes and messages, ready to pursue the business of state as the Dictator dressed.

"Now certainly this can wait today," the Dictator protested. "I am in no mood for business. Can't you see that I am in no mood for business?"

"Some business. Some will wait; some will not wait."

They walked together into his dressing room. While he dressed with the help of two attendants, he glanced at some of the business that called for his attention.

"This can wait," he said. "This certainly can wait. I find

it most provoking to be bothered with this kind of thing when I say I don't want to be bothered. Here is a petition for a street car concession from that fat pig Ginetti. We informed him what it would cost him. He pretends not to have heard us, and to have no idea of what it will cost him. That sort of behavior is trying. Send this petition back to him. Tell him I am very annoyed with him, and that he will eat the petition if he doesn't listen to what I say. The Dutch minister can wait. The more indignities I heap upon the Dutch, the more my dislike for the Germans is satisfied. As far as Santani is concerned, I consider him a gangster. I will have nothing to do with him short of one million *lire*. That is his price for respectability, and unless he pays in thirty days, it will become two million. And here again is the case of Sacco and Vanzetti. Am I never to hear the end of this? Will I hear nothing but Sacco and Vanzetti from now until doomsday? At this point, the names make me sick. Let those communist bastards fry in hell! I tell you, the names make me sick! I don't want to hear the names again."

He finished dressing. His secretary, who had remained with him, waited patiently, and finally said,

"I understand. Nevertheless, Sacco and Vanzetti are important figures to the people."

"Tell them we have taken the matter under consideration, and will do all in our power to alleviate the severity justly meted out to the two red bastards."

They walked together toward the office, and on the way they were joined by the Minister of Labor. The secretary and the Minister of Labor, both walking a pace behind the Dictator, looked at each other, and communicated with

93

brow and eyelash. They dropped four paces behind as the Dictator entered his office, and they waited while he walked twenty paces across the lush carpeting to reach his desk. When he had seated himself and swung to face them, his countenance was dark with anger, and underneath the anger was petulance. They were hounding him. Men like these, his own servants, his own aides, his own syco- phants, had become bold enough to hound him, and in- stead of the next hour being his, to dispose of as he pleased, they were determined to make it theirs.

"Nicola Sacco and Bartolomeo Vanzetti—" the secretary began.

"The matter of those two is closed," the Dictator said firmly.

The Minister of Labor came two steps closer to the Dic- tator and said, with a mixture of prudence, wariness, and the intimacy of confidence,

"You will not be faced with this matter indefinitely, sir. Tonight, both of these men will be executed. So, to a de- gree, that finishes it. I mean to indicate that a point has come where this case will complete itself."

Unable to read clearly or fathom completely the mask of anger the Dictator wore, the Minister of Labor paused, waited, and then inquired,

"May I go on? There are some facts in connection with this case that must be noted, and some things which must be done. But perhaps you would prefer not to hear all the facts?"

"Continue," the Dictator said shortly.

"Yes. As I said, the matter ends tonight. Both of these

men will be executed tonight, and then, whatever the aftermath, it will very quickly die away. It is impossible to conduct an agitational campaign for the dead. The stability of death prevents such a campaign from being effective. Nothing can really be changed by such a campaign, for death is unchangeable."

"How do you know that the execution will not be postponed again?" the Dictator demanded.

"I can be fairly confident of that. This morning, when the workers came out of the factories for their lunch, there was a demonstration of several thousand people in front of the American embassy. Rocks were thrown, windows were broken, and the automobile of the charge d'affaires of the French embassy, which happened to be standing in front of the American embassy, was overturned and set on fire. The police broke up this demonstration, and twenty-two of the ring leaders were arrested. Two of them, we are fairly certain, are communists. The others, however, are totally new to us and to our files, which gives an indication of how widely the Sacco and Vanzetti agitation has spread, and how cleverly it has been used. It puts the police in a most awkward position, for the defense of Sacco and Vanzetti becomes a matter of national pride and honor. There have been all too many tales of insults and indignities visited upon the Italian immigrants in America lately for the people to be indifferent to this matter. They see this thing as a matter of national honor. Therefore, I issued an order to the police to release all of those arrested, including the two whom we suspect of being communists—who, incidentally, we will keep under surveillance, so that they

95

may prove useful to us in that manner. I think you will agree, sir, that this action in this particular connection was the wisest thing which could be done."

The Dictator agreed. "Continue," he said.

"At two o'clock, I met with the American Ambassador. He is very devoted to you, and he stated that you might rest easy about this particularly bothersome matter. He said it will very soon be over, and no longer a source of trouble."

"He said that?" the Dictator inquired, his face less angry than before.

In precisely those words, in just so many words."

The Minister of Labor turned to the secretary for confirmation. "Did I not put it that way before—in those exact words?"

"In those exact words," The secretary nodded.

"You see that no friendship is wasted," the Dictator said, smiling for the first time since he had gotten off the masseur's table. "However, there are friendships and friendships. A fool builds bridges into a wilderness. A wise man cultivates those who possess influence."

"At three o'clock," the Minister of Labor continued, "I had a brief meeting, at the suggestion of the Ambassador, with one of the under-secretaries. This under-secretary informed me that you could be fairly certain that the execution would be carried out. He said he realized that the whole question of this pending execution placed *il Duce* and his government in a most difficult position. He wished me to assure you that all parties fully appreciate the sensitivity of your position and the exceedingly delicate nature of it. He added that important people were most outspoken in their admiration for the manner in which you have dealt with it."

"You see!" the Dictator cried, emphasizing his words by pounding his clenched fist upon his desk. "You see what would have come had I followed the advice of the bullheaded pigs who know only one thing—a communist is a communist. These men have the castor-oil mentality."

He had coined a phrase as of the moment, and he smiled in spite of himself. Both the minister and the secretary also smiled. It was really a very good and pungent phrase.

"The castor-oil mentality," the Dictator repeated. "However, you do not unify a nation with a castor-oil mentality. Is it only communists who are concerned with the fate of those two red bastards? I tell you, no. I tell you, the indignities and the wrongs suffered by Sacco and Vanzetti are an affront to every Italian who loves his motherland and who cherishes liberty! Thereby, the people will understand that their leader is not insensitive to the sufferings of any Italian anywhere. The honor of Italy is sacred. You are certain that this under-secretary was telling the truth?"

"I am absolutely certain," the Minister of Labor answered. "Furthermore, at this moment a delegation from the town of Villafalletto waits upon you, and earnestly and humbly requests an audience. Villafalletto, as you know, is the town in which Vanzetti was born. His family still lives there. However, I believe that two of the delegation are from Turin."

"You have taken their names?" the Dictator asked, his manner changed, his anger gone and now replaced with a fatherly benevolence.

"We have their names and finger prints, and already

97

we have started an investigation of them, of their associations and of their backgrounds. When they leave here, they will be under surveillance twenty-four hours a day."

"Very wise and exceedingly competent," the Dictator nodded. "A lack of thorough technical competence is a curse of our people, and I am pleased to see such understanding displayed on your part. Be certain of one thing—that when a delegation is assembled and travels hundreds of miles to see me, there are communists somewhere in the picture. Every person on the delegation is touched with the rotten filth of communism. Remember that. Now I will see them."

When the delegation entered the great office of the Dictator, he rose from his desk, walked slowly around it, and advanced to meet them, both hands outstretched, his dark eyes filled with sympathetic understanding of what faced Italy on this day; and in his countenance, sorrow appeared to mirror their own grief. The delegation was led by an old man who, it was plain to see, had worked with his hands all his life.

The Dictator extended his own hands to greet this old man, and remained for a moment in deep silence. The old worker who led the delegation took his written plea out of his pocket and unfolded it carefully. While the others stood behind him, their caps in their hands, he read hesitantly and not without fear, in a trembling voice, the following message:

"A thousand peasants and working people of Italy have gathered together in the town of Villafalletto, where Bartolomeo Vanzetti was born. We have met together in the memory of a good and gentle Italian, who is unjustly doomed to die. We resolve that we will do all in our power to prevent his death; whereupon, we humbly send a delegation of our members gathered from the villages around Villafalletto, as well as from the city of Turin, to plead with *il Duce* that he may intervene with the government of the United States to prevent this unspeakable legal murder. We know the power of *il Duce's* voice, and we humbly and respectfully urge that his voice be raised to ask clemency for two sons of our working class, Nicola Sacco and Bartolomeo Vanzetti."

When the old man had finished reading, his rheumy and tired eyes filled with tears, and he groped in his pocket for a handkerchief to dry his cheeks. Unquestionably, he had a personal relationship to the doomed men.

When the Dictator suddenly embraced the old man, everyone in the room was visibly moved by the impulsive action. Half of the delegation were weeping when they left the office, and as the Dictator reseated himself behind his desk, he himself was not unmoved. Still caught in the spirit of the occasion, he called for a stenographer, and dictated the following press release:

"*Il Duce* has communicated with the President of the United States in a plea that the lives of Nicola Sacco and Bartolomeo Vanzetti, both of them of Italian origin, may be spared. He has called upon the President of the United States to take this step in view of cementing relations between Italy and the United States, within the framework of warm friendship existing between these countries for so many years.

"The President of the United States, acknowledging *il Duce's* message, has conveyed his intense regrets that, due to the system of government prevailing in the United States, this matter would have to remain in the hands of the State government of the Commonwealth of Massachusetts. While the President of the United States recognizes the sincere interest and deep concern of *il Duce* in this matter, he regretfully announces that he has no power to intervene."

When he had finished with this message, the Dictator pointed out to the Minister of Labor that it must coincide with a statement from Washington, and that his confirmation should be obtained before his own statement was released to the press. The Minister of Labor assured him that no difficulties would lie in the path of such a desirable conclusion to the affair.

All this had acted as a catharsis, and the pall of gloom lifted from the Dictator. In another twenty minutes, he was able to leave his office for his bedroom, and suddenly the day, the future, all the circumstances of his existence, had once again become bright and joyful.

Chapter 8

BEGINNING in the morning of August 22nd, the picket line had been moving back and forth in front of the State House. The size of this picket line varied. When it began for today, there were no more than a handful of persons who defiantly and self-consciously moved along the sidewalk, walking silently in those very early hours of the day. A little later, when people began to hurry by to their work, the size of the picket line increased; and there was a brief interval around noontime when it was swelled by many men and women who joined it for fifteen minutes or a half-hour before they in turn went back to their jobs.

But even apart from this, the picket line had increased substantially by ten o'clock, and by this time, dozens of policemen had taken their places on the scene, spreading out—in effect, surrounding the picket line and attempting to give an impression of sturdy defenders of the people meeting a dangerous menace. First there were only city police; then the city police were reinforced by state police; then a car parked about a block away, four men with tommy guns sitting inside of it, ready if the occasion arose; although what possible occasion could call them into action, no one on the picket line was able to say. The actual purpose of the massed police and semi-military preparations around the picket line was more to intimidate than to defend; and in this process of intimidation, the police were not wholly unsuccessful.

For three or four days, people concerned about the Sacco-Vanzetti case had been coming into Boston from all over the United States. When the final decision was made by the Governor of the Commonwealth that Sacco and Vanzetti must go to their death at midnight of August 22nd, it seemed to many people in many parts of the United States that they themselves could hear the low but bitter moan of anguish that arose out of Boston. This was felt by an amazing variety of people. Physicians and housewives and steel workers and poets and writers and railroad engineers, and even ranch hands riding on their lonely work in the far, far west, shared this peculiar and fearful intimacy with the lives and the hopes and the fears of Sacco and Vanzetti. Execution is as old as mankind, and unquestionably the number of those who were innocent but went to their death, was great; yet never before in this land had an impending execution affected and shaken so many people.

In Seattle, Washington, the day before August 22nd, a Negro Methodist minister preached a sermon on the case of Sacco and Vanzetti. He began his sermon by recalling an experience he had had in the state of Alabama as a little child. Such experiences were common enough to Negroes born and raised in the South for a particular chord to be struck among his listeners; and the preacher went on to tell how, in the little town where he had lived, a cry for blood had filled the air. A poor, foolish, hysterical woman raised the cry that she had been raped; and then all the hounds of hell began to gallop at full pace. Even though he was just a little boy at the time, this Negro minister had consciously watched a web of circumstances tighten around an innocent man until finally the innocent man was lynched. The preacher now recalled the inevitability of these circumstances, and the anguish and suffering of the man trapped by them.

"What do I see in this case of Sacco and Vanzetti?" he asked from his pulpit. "I try to talk to you, my flock, as a man of God, which is not an easy thing. But I must also talk to you as a black man. No more can I shed my skin then I can shed, here in this life, my soul. I have been thinking a great, great deal about this case of Sacco and Vanzetti, telling myself that a Sunday would come when I could no longer keep silent and I would have to preach my sermon on it. I do not delude myself into believing that one sermon spoken by one voice will really alter the awful fate that awaits these two poor men. Neither can I delude myself into believing that my own silence should be justified by this understanding.

"Last night, I talked with my wife and my children of Sacco and Vanzetti. The five of us sitting there, all colored people whose crust of bread has at times been bitter indeed, found ourselves weeping. Afterwards, I asked myself why we had wept. I recalled that there have been those historians recently who claim that they cannot find spelled out in history, proof of the passion of our Lord, Jesus

Christ. How foolish these people are! They seek for evidence of one Christ and one crucifixion, when the history of that time tells the story of ten million crucifixions. Yesterday I and my people were slaves in bondage; and two thousand years ago, there was an angry slave called Spartacus, who led his people against their bondage, and told them to rise up and make themselves free. When he was defeated, six thousand of his followers were crucified by the Romans. Who, then, will say to me that history makes no mention of the passion of Jesus Christ?

"And will someone a thousand years from today seek vainly in the pages of history to discover and reveal the passion of Sacco and Vanzetti? Will they ask for chapter and verse—and if they should not find it, say that the Son of Man never died for us? This I asked myself, and when I had asked myself this, a bleak sadness came over me, my heart became heavy, and when I stared into the darkness, looking for light and for a pathway, none appeared. Then I had to say to myself, *You are a man of little faith and less understanding,* and I had to berate myself and become angry with myself, for in so short a time I had forgotten that I and my wife and my three children all wept because these two Italian immigrants must die, because a web of circumstances had closed about them, and no force in the whole world seems able to save them. If out of this, I see only the darkness, then indeed I have ceased to believe either in God or in His Son, our Lord, Jesus Christ.

"But always, the glimmer of light appears somehow out of the darkness. I wanted to preach a sermon, and I asked myself, who will I preach to? In my mind's eye, I saw my

104

congregation sitting in their pews, and I looked upon them in a way I had not looked upon them before. I had never said to myself before that I preach to plain working people, to hewers of wood and drawers of water. I tried to think of them only as people—and what need to define them as working people? Yet my own people are working people—are they not? I see now that you wipe your eyes. That is right. And in due time, you will weep; for the passion of Sacco and Vanzetti is your passion and mine. It is the passion of the working people of our time, whether their skin be white or black. It is the passion of the poor driven Negro of my childhood, who was hanged up by his neck by a mob of screaming, hate-driven men. It is the passion of a working man who goes from place to place, pleading that someone will buy the power of his hands, because his wife and his children are hungry. It is the passion of the Son of God, who was a carpenter.

"We are a patient people. With what effort we learned our patience, I cannot possibly estimate—for how does one measure blood and tears and heartache? But we are a patient people, and slow to anger. Yet now I do not know whether this is a virtue or a fault? They have said now that Sacco and Vanzetti must die in a few days. I do not know what our duty is, so few of us and so far away. There was one man, Peter, who could not see his Lord and companion taken, whereupon he drew a sword and smote with it. Then said Jesus unto Peter,

"'Put up thy sword into the sheath: the cup which my father hath given me, shall I not drink it?'

"Long did I ponder upon these words, trying to dispute with something within me which said, *No, this is not enough.* I have no answers. My heart is filled with sorrow, and I come to you with my sorrow to ask that we pray together for these two men. They will die for us. . . ."

These words spoken by the preacher were an expression of what some people felt, and what others felt was expressed in other ways. Many, out of the depth of their feeling, decided to journey to Boston. Most of those who did this, came without any clearly preconceived plan of what they might accomplish. Deep within themselves, as within the Negro minister, there was a need and a desire to give sound in a mighty voice; but for that kind of rage and anger and protest, people must be disciplined and trained, and these people were neither disciplined nor trained for this sort of thing. Some of those who came to Boston were poets who knew that here was an anguish beyond their command of words; others were physicians, who sensed that here was a pain and an illness that no skill of theirs could heal; and still others, who were workers, sensed even more deeply that they themselves had been sentenced to death, and that man must not die without protest. Coming to Boston, these people went to protest meetings; they asked questions to which there were no simple or definitive answers; and most of them sooner or later turned their steps toward the State House where a picket line had been in motion for many days.

Some of them could not bring themselves to join the picket line. It was no small thing to step across the crevice of fear and wonder and habit and inhibition into the ranks of a picket line. Many of these people who had come to Boston had never before in all their lives seen a picket line, much less marched on one; it was new to them. They were not certain what it meant, what its intent was, or what it might possibly accomplish; and on the part of some of them, there was a feeling that all this was a little ridiculous, this marching to and fro, carrying signs, calling out slogans, and in effect, mumbling a prayer into the thin air, a bitter prayer that two men might not perish wretchedly. Therefore, some of these people could not bring themselves to join with the picket line. Though they willed their bodies to move toward it, a stronger counter-force overcame this subjective willing, and they stood paralyzed in a dim and heartsick awareness of what their paralysis meant, and of how many more than themselves it was symbolic. Not alone were some of those who had journeyed to Boston paralyzed, but millions like them who had not come to Boston, were also paralyzed, and thereby ineffectual, and would only weep impotent tears when an Italian shoemaker and an Italian fish peddler perished at last.

There were others, however, who were not paralyzed, who managed to push aside their own reluctance, and who stepped forward and took their places in the picket line.

"Lo and behold," some of these said to themselves, "I have discovered a new weapon that I never dreamed of! A fine, strong weapon which I can use as well as another!"

They touched shoulders with people they had never seen before, and a current of strength flowed from shoulder to shoulder. Some of these people were young; others were of middle age and some were old; but all of them were alike in that they were doing something they had never done before and thereby discovered strength they had never possessed before. Many of them joined the picket line sheepishly, marched timidly at first, then more con-

fidently, then with a new bearing which denoted pride and
determination. They squared their shoulders, lifted their
heads and straightened their spines. Pride and anger
became a part of their being, and those who had remained
empty handed at first, found themselves eagerly taking
picket signs from others who had carried the signs for
hours. The signs became weapons; they were armed, and
they had a feeling, implicit if not wholly defined, that in
this simple, almost ordinary act of marching together in
protest with their fellow men and women, they had linked
themselves with a mighty movement that stretched over
the entire earth. New thoughts formed in their minds, and
new emotions surged through them; their hearts beat
faster; they knew sorrow in a way they had not known it
before, and plain anger within them was turned into
protest.

Again and again, the police engineered provocation
against the picket line. During the first part of that day of
August 22nd, the line was twice broken up, and each time,
men and women were arrested and carted away to local
police stations. This too was a new experience for many
of those on the picket line: poets, writers, lawyers, small
business men and engineers and painters who had lived
all their lives in peace and enormous security, suddenly
found themselves being handled and pushed and crowded
like common criminals, their security gone and shattered,
the law which had so long enfolded them protectingly,
now a weapon of murderous anger turned against them.
Some of these people were terribly frightened; others,
however, met anger with anger and hatred with hatred,
and in the very act of being arrested, underwent a change

that was to be with them and to affect them for all the rest of their lives.

For the workers who were arrested, the process was much simpler, for neither surprise nor fear accompanied what was to them a process neither new nor extraordinary. One of these people was a Negro worker, a sweeper from a textile mill in Providence, Rhode Island. He had taken this day off, the whole day, without pay, so that he might come to Boston and see what other people were doing, people who, like himself, could not bear the thought that death unopposed would overtake Sacco and Vanzetti. This Negro worker had not thought too much or too deeply about the case of Sacco and Vanzetti, but for many years it had been a part of his consciousness and of the world around him in a simple and direct manner. He had never combed through the evidence in the case, but now and again he would read something that either Sacco or Vanzetti had said, or something else that was a part of their backgrounds or which illuminated a part of their backgrounds; and reading this, he would understand, also in a simple and uncomplicated manner, that these two accursed men could not commit a crime, but were plain and ordinary working people like himself. Sometimes, indeed, he pondered with aching thoughtfulness over this identity, as when he read in a newspaper the following statement by Vanzetti in one of his published letters:

"Our friends must speak loudly to be heard by our murderers, our enemies have only to whisper and even be silent to be understood."

The Negro had pondered for a long time over these few words, and they had in time become a part of his own

109

decision. His decision took him, on August 22nd, to Boston, where he joined the picket line in front of the State House. He did not over-rate or under-rate this action; he recognized it for what it was, a very small action that would neither split the world asunder nor free the two men whom he had thought of for a long time as his friends. But all of his life, this man had fought against his own extinction, and had done his fighting with just such small and apparently hopeless actions, and he knew, through a wealth of practical experience, that to disdain such small actions was to disdain all action. He lived in no exalted dreams of what might be for himself tomorrow, but moved instead in terms of direct practicality for today.

In the hours he marched on the picket line, he was able to convey something of himself to the men and women around him. He was not a very tall man, but in the hard bulk of him there was an appearance of stamina and reassuring solidness. He had a square, pleasant face, and none of his motions or actions ever became either hurried or uncontrolled; and for these very reasons, he radiated an impression of his strength and conveyed to the people around him an added sense of security. He also walked easily on this task, as did many of the other workers, accepting the picket line as neither a rare nor an extraordinary moment in his existence. On the first occasion that the police tried to demolish the picket line and provoke arrests, he steadied the people around him, passed the word along, "Easy does it. Pay them no mind, and just let's us go on with our business," and thereby helped the people on the line to maintain both their discipline and their composure. However, these slow and deliberate actions of his caught the attention of the police. Plain clothes men pointed him out to each other, whereupon, he was noted and marked, and his importance was assessed. In the small struggle and drama of the picket line, he was chosen for elimination; and the second police provocation was directed toward him. He was picked up and arrested, and at one o'clock in the afternoon on August 22nd, he was brought to police headquarters and put into a cell by himself.

This distinction and special treatment troubled him. He was one of almost thirty people who had been arrested, and among them were white shoe workers and white textile workers, housewives, a famous playwright from New York City, and a poet of international reputation; but all of them had been left together. Why, then, had he been separated from them and put by himself?

It was not long before his question was answered. Since this was the very last day before the execution, time was measured in hours or even in minutes, and therefore, whatever was going to happen, could not be too long delayed. He sensed this. He was in the cell only a little while before they came for him, and then they brought him into a room where a number of people awaited him. In this room were two policemen in uniform, two other policemen in plain clothes, and an agent of the Justice Department. Also in this room there was a male stenographer, who sat at one side of the room at a desk, his pad open in front of him, waiting for whatever might develop, for whatever sounds of agony or confession he might have to set down. The two policemen in plain clothes held, each of them, a length of rubber hose, twelve inches of hose an inch in diameter, and as he entered, he saw that they were bending

111

the pieces of hose back and forth; and he had only to look at the hose, to look at the faces of the men in the room, to look at the drab bareness and ugliness of the room to which they had brought him, to know what awaited him. He was an ordinary and a rather simple man, this Negro worker, and when he understood what awaited him, his heart sank and he filled up with fear. His whole body tensed; he twisted himself from side to side, less in an attempt to escape than in involuntary and spasmodic protest of his physical being. Then the men in the room smiled at him, and he knew what their smiles meant.

The representative of the Justice Department explained to him why they had brought him there.

"You see," he said to the Negro, "we don't want to make any trouble for you. We certainly don't want to cause you any pain or misery. We want to ask you some questions and we want you to answer them truthfully. If you do that, you have nothing at all to worry about, and you will be released in just a little while. That is why we have brought you here—to answer these questions. You are an honest man, aren't you, and a good American?"

"I am a good American," the Negro replied earnestly.

The two plain clothes men stopped bending the rubber hose, and they both smiled at him. Both of them had wide, thin-lipped mouths; it made them look almost like brothers. They smiled easily and without any difficulty, but also without any humor.

"If you are a good American," said the man from the Justice Department, "then we won't have any trouble at all, not one bit of trouble. What we want to know is one simple fact—who paid you to march on that picket line?"

"Nobody paid me," the Negro answered.

Whereupon, the two plain clothes men stopped smiling, and the Justice Department man shrugged his shoulders rather regretfully. He stopped being as friendly as he had been before, but he was still not unfriendly.

"What's your name?" he asked the Negro worker.

The Negro told him. The Justice Department man asked him to repeat what he had said a little louder, so that the stenographer could get it. The Negro did this.

"How old are you?" the Justice Department man asked.

The Negro replied that he was thirty-three years old.

"Where are you from?" the Justice Department man inquired.

The Negro told him he was from Providence, and he had come to Boston that same morning on the New York, New Haven and Hartford train.

"Do you work in Providence?" the Justice Department man asked.

With this question, the Negro knew that it was no use at all for him to hope. No matter what he did from here on, he could not change things materially. If he did not tell them where he worked, they would find it out in their own good time and in their own good way, and in the process of finding it out, the music would begin. He knew just what kind of melody the music would play, and he knew who would dance and who would pay the pipers. He was afraid, and not ashamed to admit the fact to himself; and now he put off the final reckoning for a moment; let the music play later. He told them where he worked and they noted it down. He knew he would never work there again. He knew he would never work anywhere in this part of the country again. He had a wife and a three year old daughter, and because of this, there was an added sadness and poignancy in his knowing that he would never work anywhere in this part of the country again. But still, it was happening, and there was nothing at all that he could do about it except to let it happen. It was happening, but it had only begun to happen; and it would go on happening now.

"Why did you come to Boston?" the Justice Department man asked pleasantly enough.

"I came because I don't think Sacco and Vanzetti should just die like this, with no word or action of protest."

"Do you think that by coming here you could prevent them from dying?"

"No, sir, I don't think that."

"Then if you don't think that, you are just contradicting yourself, and nothing you say makes any sense. Does it make any sense to you?"

"Yes, sir, it does."

"Suppose you tell me how it makes sense to you."

"Well, sir, either I could do nothing, or I could come up here to Boston and see if maybe there wasn't something to do, something that I might do about them two poor folks."

"Like what?"

"Like marching in the picket line today."

The Justice Department man said, his voice suddenly high-pitched and angry, "God damn it now, you are a liar! I sure don't like to be lied to by a boy like you! It's not doing yourself any good to lie."

Then the Justice Department man sat down in a wooden chair, and the two plain clothes men sat down on an old table at one side of the room. The two policemen in uniform walked over to the closed door and stood, one on each side of it, leaning against the door frame. This made a little current of movement in the room, and the Negro worker was acutely aware of this current, and very sensitive to it, for he knew that this current meant that they were through with the first part of their intentions toward him, and would now begin with the second part. They left him standing alone for a while, but they all looked at him. He knew what it meant when many white men looked at you in just that way. Now he thought of his wife and child, and he was overcome with great sadness, just as if someone close to him had died. He realized that this was because death was in the air. They had intended him to understand that death was in the air.

"I just think you are lying," the man from the Justice Department said. "We want you to tell the truth. If you lie to us, it's going bad with you. If you tell the truth, we can all be good friends. Now, I think that someone organized you up here to Boston. I also think that someone paid you to walk on that picket line. That's what we want you to tell us—who organized you up here, and who paid you to go out there and picket? Now, you might feel that whoever did that was a friend of yours, but you are pretty foolish if you feel that way. Just look around you now, and you can see that whoever got you into this was no friend of yours. He certainly wasn't doing anything to do you any good, so you certainly have no obligation to him. The very best thing you can do is to tell us the truth about who he was and what he paid you."

"Oh, Lord," the Negro thought. "Oh, Lord God, this is going to be a trying thing." And then he shook his head and said no, no one had paid him. He had just come here on his own, no one had told him to do it; he just did it because he knew about Sacco and Vanzetti, and felt very deeply what suffering they had been through. He also tried to explain that one of the reasons why he had come to Boston was that Sacco and Vanzetti were just plain and ordinary working people like himself; but when he began to explain this, they moved in on him and beat him, so that the words were lost and they never heard that part of his story.

They did not beat him very much now. The two plain clothes men came up to him, one from the side and one from behind him. The one from behind him let him feel the hose back and forth across his kidneys, whipping it hard; and when he pulled away from him, crying out with the pain, the other plain clothes man hit him with the rubber hose across the face, the nose and the eyes, so that his eyes filled with tears and pain, and his nose began to bleed. He backed away, making little noises of pain, and they did not follow him. He saw the blood running down his shirt, and he took a handkerchief out of his pocket and wiped the blood away, and then he pressed the handkerchief to his nose. His back, where they had beaten him over the kidneys, hurt a great deal, and his head hurt from the blow across the eyes. He saw everything through a haze, and his eyes were full of tears, nor did the tears stop coming.

"Let's say this," said the Justice Department man. "Let's say that you will be cooperative with us, and then we won't beat you? My goodness, that's the last thing in the world we want. Did you know that someone tried to throw a bomb into the judge's house? Can you imagine that! Here is a judge in a lawful court in this Commonwealth and these United States, and these two sons-of-bitches, Sacco and Vanzetti, come up before him and he does his honorable and Constitutional duty of hearing the evidence and weighing the evidence and then passing sentence. Why, such a man is the rock and the pillar of our lives, of your life as well as my life. You would think, wouldn't you, that for such a man there would be hosannas of praise. But this is by no means the case. Instead of praise, people organize a bomb-throwing because he sentenced these two red bastards. Don't you think that bomb-throwing is a terrible business?"

The Negro nodded, and agreed. Yes, he thought so. He thought people who threw bombs, who took life, who murdered and brutalized, were doing terrible things indeed.

"Well, now, I am glad that you feel that way," the agent said. "It's going to make everything a lot simpler, because you feel that way. You see, we think we know who threw that bomb. We also think you know. I am going to spell out what I know, and all you have to do is agree to what I know and put your name to it. That means you are bearing lawful witness for the State, and being a good American. Then we let you go. Then we don't trouble you one bit."

"But I don't know," the Negro worker said. "How can I sign anything if I don't know? Then I would be signing a lie. I don't want to lie about such a thing; it's a serious thing."

This last was evidently amusing to everyone except the Justice Department agent. The two plain clothes men smiled; the two policemen in uniform also smiled. Only the Justice Department man remained serious and somber, for there was work to be done.

When the work was finished, they carried the Negro to a cell and laid him down inside the cell on a cot. It was there that the Professor of Criminal Law saw him. The Professor of Criminal Law was one of a fairly large number of lawyers who were either attached to the case or had volunteered their services in the Sacco-Vanzetti case. But today, on August 22nd, every one of these lawyers was up to his ears in work, in last minute things, desperate things with shreds of hope, petitions, pleas for a stay of execution, various actions on behalf of people who had been arrested for picketing or arrested for other forms of protest.

The white people who were arrested on the picket line today were worried about what had happened to the Negro, and they informed the Defense Committee that a Negro on the picket line had been put away somewhere by the police, and the Defense Committee asked the Professor of Criminal Law whether he would see what he could do about the case. He said he would, and if the truth be told, he was grateful for the opportunity to do something even so peripherally; for he found waiting helplessly, or indeed any sort of inactivity on this day, absolutely unendurable. He got a writ of habeas corpus, and he went to the police station and demanded to see the Negro. They knew who he was, and they knew that his reputation was not inconsiderable, and therefore the captain of police himself sought out the Justice Department agent and spoke to him about what they should do. He said to him,

"It's that Jew lawyer from the University, and he wants to see your black boy or make a stink about it. He's got a writ."

"I don't think he ought to see him," the Justice Department man answered.

A lieutenant of detectives standing by, said, "You cookies come here from Washington, and you come and you go just as free as birds on the wing. We have to live with this city. Tomorrow, the case of Sacco and Vanzetti is maybe over, but we are still earning our daily bread in Boston. What are you going to do with this black boy? Freeze him? Put him on ice for the rest of his natural life? Let the lawyer see him. What the hell is the difference? Nobody's going to sound off over a jig being pushed around a little."

"He don't look very good," the police captain protested mildly.

"Oh, what the hell! Maybe he didn't look so good to start. Let this Jew-boy make a stink about it. Who gives a damn? Nobody's going to wave any banner for no jig."

So the lawyer was let in, and he stood in the cell where the Negro worker lay stretched out on the bed, his face all beaten to a bloody pulp, his eyes closed, his nose broken, and the blood welling from between cracked lips. He lay there moaning and groaning and whimpering, and the Professor of Criminal Law tried to comfort him in some way and reassure him and explain to him that now

119

it was only a matter of an hour or two before he would be released.

"I am sure grateful to you for this, mister," the Negro said. "It's only because I got such awful pain that I can't properly talk to you and express my gratitude. Also, they closed my eyes and I am just filled with fear that I won't be able to see again."

"You will be able to see again," the Professor of Criminal Law said. "I am going to get you a doctor now. Don't worry about that. Why did they do it?"

"I wouldn't sign no confession about knowing a man who they say threw a bomb," the Negro answered slowly and painfully. "I don't know nobody who throws bombs, and I just don't believe them. They're framing somebody, and I couldn't just, in the sight of God and my own self, make a liar out of myself."

"No, you couldn't," said the Professor of Criminal Law, his voice sad and bitter. "Now, take it easy. I am going to get a doctor for you, and as I said, in a few hours you will be out of here and it will all be over."

Chapter 9

IT WAS about two o'clock in the afternoon of August 22, 1927, that the President of the United States was informed of a rather simple request made of him by the Dictator of Fascist Italy. The Dictator wondered whether clemency of a sort might not be found for two "wretched and unfortunate Italians, under sentence of death by the Commonwealth of Massachusetts." Time was running out, and the very imminence of their death had led the Dictator to approach the President directly. At the same time, the representatives of the State Department who discussed this matter with the President at his ranch house where he was vacationing, made it plain that this formality had been forced upon the Dictator of Italy by great mass pressure. It was common knowledge that among those least loved by the Dictator, were radicals of any sort, and that he would hardly shed tears over the death of Nicola Sacco and Bartolomeo Vanzetti.

The President had a reputation for thoughtfulness, and his tendency toward long and unbearable silences bolstered this reputation. Somehow or other, it is never accepted as a possibility that people who habitually say little, may take this course because the bleakness of their inner lives gives them very little to say. Silence is far more often the result of emptiness than fullness; but folklore has wrapped it in a mantle of wisdom. In any case, it makes sense that a man does not become President without varied virtues, and naturally this must have been the case with this President. He had thin lips, small eyes, and a long sharp nose; his pinched face was neither gentle nor winning, and his voice was as sharp and rasping as his personality. If he lacked other graces, he must of necessity have had wit. Some people looked in vain for it, but others claimed to have found it, and they characterized him as *gnome-like.* The word was unfamiliar, and people who had at long last discovered why this man was President, pronounced the *g.* Whereupon, the newspapers, which had taken to calling the President *gnomic,* pointed out that the *g* was silent, and that the word rhymed with the name of the Alaskan town. It was *gnomic* when the President said,

"The left and the right hands move as the body moves, and if the body is threatened, they defend it together. So with the left and the right in politics."

The press liked this kind of thing, but the President's intimates heard him talk otherwise. He was a New Englander, born in Vermont, but raised up in Massachusetts, where he once broke a police strike. He was Governor of the State of Massachusetts at that time, a time when the Boston policemen had been driven beyond endurance by the hunger of their children and the prodding of their wives, who intimated that they were less than men, for even a dog will move against hunger and thirst. So that almost unheard-of thing took place, a police strike; and the country caught the drama of the practically unprecedented situation and blew it up all out of proportion. Into this situation, the man who was now President moved, doing a series of uninspired and obvious things—yet thereafter, it was remembered that he had broken the police strike.

"Do you remember," the present Governor of the Commonwealth was to say not too much later on this same day, "how he broke the police strike? There was a demonstration of firmness and decision rare in a public servant—something to emulate. I am thinking more of that noble precedent than of what people will say about me that might redound to my discredit."

The truth of the matter was that this present Governor was thinking that now in the White House sat a man who was once Governor of this same State. Who was to say that it could not happen again? In any case, an undeviating hatred of anything that was red, tinted red, faintly red or pink or anything like that, would be a very firm and reliable guide. It is said that most men want to be President.

The man who was President, however, said little about anything. Whenever he was confronted with a situation which he could not wholly comprehend, or a decision which he could not comfortably make, he took refuge in his silence. On this day, on this August 22nd, the representative of the State Department, facing him, tried to recall exactly what the attitude of the White House toward the case of Sacco and Vanzetti really was—and then he recalled that in all truth, there was no attitude of the White House. The White House had been of no opinion whatsoever.

"Of course I cannot intervene," the President now said.

"No?"

"I feel sympathetic toward *il Duce's* problem—" He left it there, hanging in the air. A stenographer sat at one side of his huge and ornate desk, but it did not seem that he intended to dictate anything. His small eyes were undisturbed, placid, perhaps contemplative of the vastness of the nation he headed, the land he ruled, where a smooth and well-oiled machine of government and society functioned. Always, on every day, people like these two, like Sacco and Vanzetti, communists, agitators and labor organizers, were caught in the tight gears of that machine. Nothing satisfied them but to be so caught, it would seem. But then they squealed so loud and painfully. . . .

"*Il Duce's* difficulty is understandable. Since the two men are Italian, it does present a question of national honor, which the communists there will make the most of. There have been a number of rather large demonstrations, Turin, Naples, Genoa, Rome." The representative of the State Department ruffled through his papers. He had come well armed with index and reference. He explained that what he now read was from *Il Popolo*, and added, "not entirely an unofficial opinion, Mr. President—"

"I never really understood how close a hand he has on his press."

"Quite close. Nothing like it in our experience. A newspaper editor who talks out of turn can shortcut the inevitability of what will follow, and blow out his brains. The

124

fascists are very orderly, and he likes to keep a finger in everything. Well, here they say, 'America has administered the justice of liberty, first among all goddesses, so the decision in court cannot and must not be discussed—' You see, orderly people; that is a signature of fascism, 'but justice and liberty served, we believe an act of mercy now would be opportune, just and wise.' Well, one cannot simply take that at face value either. It strengthens *il Duce* to have such an editorial as that in his paper—makes the people say, well, there he is, for every Italian. On the other hand, he does not challenge the trial and decision—only mercy is pleaded for. It does sound a little hypocritical, when you think of how many communists he has put away, firing squads and prison, detention camps, and castor oil—"

The President was curious about the castor oil. "I keep hearing about it. Just what is it?"

"As nearly as we can find out, a way of treating reds. They are trussed up, their mouths are forced open, and a quart or so of castor oil is poured down their gullets. It sounds horrible, and probably feels like the very devil; but I suppose they had to resort to that kind of thing to shake them up a little."

"He shook them up," the President agreed. "He made the trains run on time. But none of them seem to understand us. A State is a State. A President can't interfere. Let him know that I can't interfere. It must run through, and tonight it will be over. I can't go into Massachusetts and tell the Governor what to do. They've had a fair trial and more than enough time to review the facts—"

His voice trailed away. He had said a good deal, for

him. He didn't get angry, but the representative of the State Department knew that he didn't like reds of any description. They were all trouble makers, yet there had to be some significance to all the trouble that was being made anywhere and everywhere. He had to be informed. The crowd outside the American embassy in London right now must include ten or fifteen thousand people. He had a report on that only a few minutes before he came here.

"They don't like us," the President said shortly.

"Demonstrations day and night in France, twenty-five thousand in Paris, Toulouse, Lyons, Marseilles. Germany— a very big demonstration in Berlin, and in Frankfort and Hamburg—"

The President seemed unconcerned. His face registered neither amazement nor disbelief. The thunder of a million marching workers, the shattering sound of their feet on the streets of Moscow and Peking and Calcutta and Brussels, the plea of their delegates, the fierce anger of their protest—all of it died to a whisper here.

"It is not a matter of concern for the administration," the President said.

"The Secretary of State thought you ought to know about the situation in Latin America. They are very restive there."

"I don't see what the devil concern of theirs it is," the President remarked bluntly, causing the man from the State Department to wonder whether any human being could be so impervious to currents and forces; unconcern was one thing—this kind of indifference, however, passed belief. He detailed his report—strikes, protest meetings, marching anger, windows in embassies and consulates smashed, Colombia, Venezuela, Brazil, Chile, the Argentine—yes, and a devil of an outburst in South Africa.

"South Africa—really?" the President said.

"The reports from the legations are quite nervous. Suddenly the whole world is screaming at us in rage."

Now the President smiled, not with humor but with the first evidence of disbelief he had yet exhibited. "Really? It's a most peculiar thing. I suppose the Russians are in it somewhere. Otherwise, how can you explain all this hue and cry over two agitators?"

"I can't explain it, sir. However, the British embassy feels that some effort should be taken with the Governor of Massachusetts to have the execution postponed."

The President shook his head. "They've had a fair trial."

"Yes—"

"I have no inclination to interfere."

The representative of the State Department put his papers back into his portfolio and left. The President dismissed his stenographer and sat alone for a little while. His thoughts moved in their courses, orderly courses. It was a very strange thing to be President of the United States. Here, even while he was on vacation, his desk remained full of business, and everything had to halt because there was such a commotion about a shoemaker and a fish peddler. Here he sat in a ranch house far from Washington, in the Black Hills of North Dakota, yet the world was at his fingertips, and at his back, a nation more prosperous and powerful than any ever dreamt of in all the history of mankind. A new prophet had arisen in this land; his name was Henry Ford, and he had devised a moving thing called an assembly line, and a Ford car dropped off the end of it every thirty seconds or so; and thoughtful men wrote essays concerning the replacement of Marxism with Fordism. In this land, there would be two cars in every garage and a chicken in every pot, and—as one bitter columnist put it—a slow and orderly development until the bathrooms had bathrooms. The hateful communist legend of cyclical depression had been hurled back into the pot of lies that spawned it; depression and crisis were gone, and the land was rich and powerful and fruitful beyond belief and, not impossibly, forever.

All this had been challenged by two ragged agitators, illiterate men thrown up by the Mediterranean Basin, that breeding place of dark folk with dark souls—so different from and unpleasant to the Anglo-Saxon—and these two men had come filled with hate and fury. Whereupon, the greatness of the land captured them without anger, submitting them to due process of law

And yet the world was angry and dissatisfied; and the whole world rocked with sound about these two men. It was easy to dismiss it as *Russian-made;* but the label did not solve the puzzle for the dry and sour man in the Black Hills. Nor could he take solace in hatred; he hated indifferently, and he could not think of the shoemaker and the fish peddler as human folk deserving of hatred. Dogs were muzzled and cattle were slain without hatred. . . .

His thoughts moved in their courses, orderly—pursuing a certain thread of recollection. It was not long ago, in Washington, that his secretary had entered his office softly and easily, and said,

"The Justice is here."

"Here?"

"Right outside. You had an appointment—"

"Never mind that! My word, don't you understand? Don't talk like a fool! The Justice is here—well, show him in."

The Justice was one man, unmistakably, and of course he needed no other identification. It seemed, sometimes, to more people than just the President, that all of justice and law and the memory of justice and law were wrapped up in the dry old skin of the Justice.

Then the Justice came into the office of the President. The President rose, full of words of protest about the Justice's coming, but the old man waved him back to his seat. This was an old man, indeed—an old, old man. His skin was dry as parchment; his eyes were deep in his head; his voice was resonant, yet cracked with age, for he had far better than the three-score and ten years allotted to most men. Somewhere behind his eyes was a memory of many things; with those same eyes, he had seen the guns crash at Gettysburg, the hillside carpeted with the dead, and many an hour had he spent in talk with old Abraham Lincoln. From that time to this time, how many had lived and struggled and died—and all this he had witnessed, old, old man that he was. His presence impressed even the stolid executive; the old man was old New England, and all the ancient, distant times now gone forever— stretching away back to the days when Paul Revere kept his silver shop in little Boston Town. The President looked at him strangely; for even though he was the President, it was a singular thing for this old man to call upon him.

"Now won't you please sit down?" the President asked.

It was just as hot as blazes that day in Washington, and

the Justice nodded and sat down alongside of the President's desk rather gratefully, placing his yellow straw hat upon the desk and balancing his cane between his bony knees.

"I decided to see you, sir," the Justice said, treating the fact as a prerogative rather than a privilege, "because they came to me for a stay of execution. I refer to the *Case of Nicola Sacco and Bartolomeo Vanzetti versus the Commonwealth of Massachusetts*. They have at last been sentenced to death, and the Governor has announced a date for the execution. I was asked to stay the execution. I imagine you are acquainted with the facts in the case?"

"Sufficiently," the President said.

"Yes. I have not read it too carefully, but I glanced through an essay on the case, written by a teacher of law in Boston. Usually, I frown upon such monographs which try to influence the bench with public opinion, but this one is rather cleverly done. The case has many points of interest, and it has raised something of a national and international furor. There are forces which seem desirous of presenting the two defendants as saints. When they came to me today for the stay of execution, I pointed out to them that a State legal decision may well be set aside by the Supreme Court of the United States, if the record of the case clearly shows that the Constitution has been infringed upon in certain ways. In this case, the defense has already filed an application for a *writ of certiorari* on grounds of Constitutional infringement. They also presented a *writ of habeas corpus,* which was denied. Whereupon, they approached me to grant them a stay of execution until the application for *certiorari* has been considered by the entire court. Naturally, the court cannot be convened in the summer, regardless of how extraordinary the circumstances may appear to be; yet since the execution is set for the month of August, in the normal course of things the defendants will be dead when the court considers the application. Thereby, the request for the stay. The situation, you recognize, is most unusual; and I cannot think of any precedent which could be used as a guiding principle. I can only surmise as to whether or not I possess such power under the Constitution—yet I think if the occasion demanded, I would exercise it. On my part, I cannot imagine circumstances where the court would reverse or set aside the verdict. I cannot believe it possible. Therefore, my inclination is not to grant a stay of execution. However, the matter is one of such gravity that I decided to have your opinion, and to see whether you, perhaps, might not be aware of some facts or circumstances unknown to me which would recommend a stay of execution."

"I am aware of none, sir," the President said.

"You do not feel it would bring honor to the land, as an act of judicial mercy?"

"I do not."

The old man rose to go, gravely thanking the President for his opinion—and now the President recalled this, recalled mention of the monograph written by a teacher of law in Massachusetts.

"Now where did I see his name?" the President wondered, and sought among his papers for a telegram which had come this same day. He found it, and read again,

"I humbly and respectfully beg you, sir, to consider the

131

fact that I have seen—and this I will swear to—with my own eyes, proof of the innocence of these two men. If there is even a faint chance of the validity of such evidence, must we not test it? I do not ask for mercy, but for a full measure of the law. If the law should go, what is left to us? What shield have we to defend us? What wall to shelter us? I beg you to wire the Governor of Massachusetts, asking him to postpone the day of execution. Even twenty-four hours will help—"

It was the persistence of the telegram that annoyed the President, and then he saw the name at the bottom, a name so obviously Jewish. Wasn't that the name the Justice had referred to? And why were Jews so insensitively persistent?

He put the telegram aside, handling it with distaste. It was one of dozens of telegrams he had received today. He had not replied to any, nor would he, being, as a matter of fact, sick and tired of the whole affair.

Chapter 10

THE PROFESSOR of Criminal Law was late. His appointment
with the Writer from New York City had been for three
o'clock in the afternoon; but here already it was past three
o'clock, and he had missed him at the office of the Defense
Committee. When he had inquired there, they thought
that possibly the Writer had gone over to join the picket
line in front of the State House, or on Temple Street, and
that was where the Professor of Criminal Law went to
look for him, walking down Beacon Street, and conscious
—ever more so as the day lengthened—of the two men in
the State Prison only a stone's throw away.

What a diversity of moods and what a variety of experiences he had gone through today! So much had already
happened, and without doubt so very much more was due
to happen! The consequential mixed most strangely with
the inconsequential—to a point where he sometimes thought
that every single motion, action and moment of this singular
and awful day was weighted with specific meaning in
itself. Such thoughts were not too clear, but he was aware

that he was no longer thinking very clearly; he was becoming a part of this day, and the motion, the heat, the brutality, the anger and the heartsickness had all had a profound and disturbing effect upon him—to a point where now, hurrying along through the hot summer afternoon, he found himself reciting days and dates. His experiences of the past hours had given him a feeling known to many who go through the adventure of highly concentrated events; time had telescoped; and it seemed that weeks and even months were crowded into what the calendar specified as days. Here it was only Monday afternoon, but already the Sunday of twenty-four hours ago existed in an almost forgotten past.

This kind of thinking made him wonder what time was like on this day for Sacco and Vanzetti—how the minutes marched for them, and whether the day passed slowly or quickly? He realized that he, like so many in Boston on this particular Monday, had identified himself subjectively with Sacco and Vanzetti; and therefore when he considered how the passage of time must seem to them, a cold chill of fear came over him, and suddenly he was inside of two men, looking out of the windows of their eyes and sharing with them the dreadful apprehension of approaching death. He felt his heart race and pound with fear in response to this exercise of his imagination; and he understood that he, like so many others, would die over and over again on this summer day, experiencing, time without end, the agony of the shoemaker and the fish peddler.

Unquestionably, this was the case with the Writer, and their agony was his agony; what else had brought him to Boston today? Although he had never seen the man he was now hurrying to see, the Professor of Criminal Law felt that he knew the Writer very well. On and off, for years past, he had read the Writer's newspaper columns and delighted in the man's savage irony, his endless wit, and his warm heart. Like the Professor of Criminal Law, the Writer was a man of emotion. He could be both caustic and sentimental, each to the extreme; and an awareness of this similarity in their emotional makeup made the Professor of Criminal Law a little apprehensive about their actual meeting. How strange, he thought to himself, that he should be worrying about such things on this day; yet he realized that the true content of such a day consisted of small matters as well as large matters, absurdities as well as profundities. Though the world might be at the final edge of its existence, men would still eat and drink, and their bodies would still rid themselves of waste.

Now the Professor was approaching the State House. He halted a short distance from the picket line, studying the people walking by, and there he found, unmistakably, the huge, hulking, untidy form of the Writer, a big man, fat, bear-like in his ambling gate, shaggy-haired, and wrapped in his own brooding introspection as he walked back and forth in the hot August sun. The Professor had no doubts as to whether or not this was the man he was supposed to meet, so apparently was the Writer himself and no one else. Whereupon, he went over and introduced himself, and the Writer stepped out of the line to shake the hand of the Professor of Criminal Law, referring immediately to the excellence of the monograph which the Professor had written about the case of Sacco and Vanzetti.

"I have waited to say this to you personally," the Writer

135

told him, "because you have performed a great service for me, for the two men in the death house, and for thousands of others. You have taken the heartbreaking complexity of this case and distilled out of it the simple and logical truth. I for one am most indebted."

The Professor was embarrassed—not because of the praise, but because he felt that today of all days his work should not be praised. He said something to the effect of living in a world which eschewed logic, nodding at the State House and reminding the writer,

"That is hardly a haven for the truth, nor do they welcome logic."

"No, I don't suppose they do. We are late for our appointment with the Governor, aren't we?" the Writer asked. "Has that spoiled our chances of seeing him?"

"We are a little late, but I am sure he will see us."

"I never understood why he was willing to see us in the first place. It's all at odds with the man; it's at odds with his personality."

"But, you see, he is at odds with himself today," the Professor explained. "He will see everyone he has time for today, if I am not mistaken. He will sit there in the State House and see everyone and listen to everyone, and he will not move from there until it is all over. He is experiencing his own particular trial and salvation. I think he believes that when today is over, he will be as good as President of the United States, barring only the mechanical problems of nomination and election, which still lie in the future."

The Writer watched the Professor curiously throughout this speech, wondering at the soft yet insistent note of bitterness in the man's voice; and hearing this note of bitterness, and seeing the man, the Writer thought again of the amazing complex that Boston had become on this strange summer day. Being a writer, he was called upon to observe even himself with a certain amount of objectivity; and as he and the Professor of Criminal Law went into the State House, the Writer composed in his own mind the passage of people and events into which he had plunged since he arrived in Boston a few hours ago.

"Now," he said to himself, "I am walking into the power of Massachusetts government. In this house here is a small man who has been turned for the day into a god. I must raise to myself, examine, and solve the problem of whether he is to be pitied. I have already speculated upon his wickedness. It is an ancient wickedness, and he sits in his mansion like Pharaoh of long ago, with a heart turned to stone. He is reputed to be worth over forty million dollars. In that sense, he matches Pharaoh, and more. His wealth is not less than the treasures of all Egypt. He rules the Commonwealth of Massachusetts, and while he does not possess the secret of giving life, he has the power of taking it away from those who live. He maintains all the trappings of everyday, but he is a fearsome personage. There are many wrongs here, but I wonder whether any wrong is more dreadful than that which puts the decision of life or death into the hands of one individual—"

In that way, the Writer's mind composed this part of the scene and that part of the scene, into a literary whole. It was his manner of functioning, and he could no more have prevented this creative process from taking place than he could willfully have stopped breathing. For the Professor of Criminal Law, it was different, and in him doubt and fear mixed with tiredness. When reporters gathered around them, asking questions, the Professor of Criminal Law shook his head stubbornly, and said,

"Please don't stop us now. We had an appointment with the Governor for three o'clock, and it's already late. What can we possibly tell you until after we have seen the Governor?"

"Is it true that Vanzetti's sister is coming here?" they wanted to know.

"I don't know anything about that," the Professor of Criminal Law replied; but the Writer had already broadened his picture to include a woman who had come from a distant place to plead for her brother's life, the simple, wonderful drama of it—a drama that only life could paint so boldly—taking hard hold of him.

Then they were at the Governor's office, and the Governor's secretary welcomed them politely and took them inside.

With an expression which denoted neither friendship nor hostility, the Governor of the Commonwealth of Massachusetts greeted them and examined them. The Governor sat behind his desk—a solid part of a world of small men who sat behind large desks and regarded with manner part querulous, part defensive, part eager, all those who came before them; as well he might—for these were two strange and uncomfortable men who had stepped into the seat of the ancient glory which he ruled.

At first, long, long ago, when the Pilgrim Fathers came to this land, they built their houses of rough-hewn boards; the ceilings were low, and there was a bare and proud

138

dignity in the most humble dwelling place; in time, however, they learned different ways of life, and pride parted
company with humility. The State House was old, but not
as old as those days of bare pride; and this room wherein
the Governor sat was a place of aristocratic beauty and
gilded distinction, the lintels cleverly carved, the wainscot-
ting covered with fine white enamel, and each piece of
furniture from the hand of a master. It was not such a
room that a man with forty million dollars and more would
feel ill at ease in; but the Professor of Criminal Law and
the Writer from New York City stood in it as awkwardly
as if they were both of them culprits in the eyes of the
law and prisoners before the bar.

The clothes they wore were wrinkled and stained with
perspiration. The Writer, dressed in a suit of ivory summer
cloth, seemed as painfully out of place here as a bear
would be in man's attire and man's dwelling. The Professor of Criminal Law wore his clothes poorly at best,
and now he nervously kept turning his straw hat round
and round in his damp fingers.

They had come to plead; and the Governor realized that
this they had in common with all who entered his office
today, large and small, rich and poor—people of fame or
those of no consequence in his eyes, they all came to plead,
to beg, to whine for the life of two dirty agitators, two men
of broken speech and sneaking words, two men who had
dedicated their lives to tearing down the beautiful erections
of the Governor's world. This was how the Governor saw
it, and this was the substance of what the Governor thought
as he looked at these two supplicants. He did not feel
very much emotion. For him, today was a day without

emotion, bare of it; nor was it easy for him to keep his thoughts from wandering, keep them here with him in his office in the State House, fixed on this dreary business of pleading. At the bottom of everything, he had a sound basis upon which to function; he had a goal; he knew in his own mind where he was going and what he was doing; and therefore, he had decided that he would refuse no one a word with him on this day. Let them all come and bear witness that his mind was not closed.

Whereupon, he listened. He weighed one statement against another statement. He was a patient man, a judicious man, not a cruel man. These, the Professor and the Writer, perhaps like others who had come and gone, would think of him as a cruel man; but in that they would be hitting wide of the mark. Rejection of sentimentality was hardly cruelty. How could he see his own duty, if he saw it as twenty others desired him to see it? Now as he looked at these two uncomely, unattractive men who had appeared so tardily for their appointment with him, the one a Jewish teacher, the other a newspaper writer with a reputation for eccentricity and radical leanings, he considered with a good deal of self-pity how much of a tortured and abused man he, the Governor, had become since this whole dreadful business began to reach its climax.

"Pontius Pilate," they called him, not knowing how little of a Pilate he was, he, a simple business man with gastritis, unexplained stomach pains, fear of a heart attack, and a woeful desire to do things easily and painlessly, pleasing those whose opinions he rejected. The fact that he was very rich did not necessarily mean that he was a bad man. Why, just a month ago, he had himself gone to the State Prison

140

across the river and had spoken in person to Sacco and Vanzetti. One would think that they would have been glad to see him, that they would have realized what it meant for him, the Governor of the Commonwealth, to come to a prison to visit two condemned thieves and murderers, and to hear their side of the story. But instead of demonstrating gratitude, Sacco would not even talk to him, but looked at him with eyes full of horror and contempt—so that Vanzetti had to explain apologetically, "He doesn't hate you personally, Governor, but you are a symbol of those forces he hates." "What are those forces?" "The forces of wealth and power," Vanzetti answered calmly. Then they had talked a little, and the Governor saw in Vanzetti's eyes, as he had seen before in the eyes of Sacco, anger and contempt.

The Governor never forgot or forgave that look. He had said to himself then, "All right, you damned reds—think that if you wish to."

Now supplicants for the "damned reds" came to plead. The whole world was coming to plead with the Governor. Here were a professor and a writer. Before, there had been a clergyman and a poet, and after these, two others, two women, were expected.

The Professor began with apologies for being late. He said that there were certain circumstances which had prevented their being on time, and that he regretted this tremendously, for of all appointments he had ever had, he felt that this was perhaps the most important.

"Why do you say that?" the Governor wanted to know. His ingenuous manner of speaking was not assumed. The conclusion came less quickly to the Professor of Criminal

141

Law; but almost immediately, the Writer realized that the Governor was a stupid man; and it had to be incongruous and unbelievable and in some ways more horrible than any other part of this cursed day, that a man so stupid and beyond the reach of emotion or logic should sit in the State House of the Commonwealth of Massachusetts, wielding the quick and final power of death. Therefore, much of what the eyes and the ears of this Writer told him, his civilized sense of reason found impossible to accept. Fools do not sit in the seats of the mighty, his reason assured him, nor are forty million dollars given to foolish men.

"You now have to argue a cause and plead a case," he pointed out to himself. "Therefore, do not underestimate the shrewdness of this man who sits before you."

Meanwhile, the Professor of Criminal Law had begun to speak, and was stating forcefully, albeit humbly, that he had not come here today to waste the Governor's time. He had come because the world granted that fact that he, the Professor of Criminal Law, was a little better acquainted than the average person with the facts of the case of Sacco and Vanzetti, because he had interested himself deeply in those facts over a period of many years, and because those facts clamored for certain new arguments. In this initial presentation of his statement, the Professor appeared to be almost abject in his bearing; and the Writer wondered how a man could be both humble and earnest to such an extent. Causation and motivation of people were, if not the bread, then at least the butter of this Writer's process of living, and he was as curious to know what terrible necessity drove the Professor of Criminal Law as he was to know what grim urge to take two lives rode the Governor.

"I want to be patient," the Governor said, "but you must understand that for days now, people have been seeking me out and stating that they either had new evidence or importantly new interpretations of old evidence. I have heard their statements with what I may say is extraordinary patience, but nowhere have they been able to demonstrate that any of the evidence they presented to me was new evidence, or evidence that could radically change my approach to the case. As the result of my study of the record and my personal investigation of the case, including my interviews with a large number of witnesses, I believe with the jury that Sacco and Vanzetti were guilty, and that their trial was fair. The crime for which they are to pay, was committed seven years ago. For six years, through dilatory methods, one appeal after another, every possibility for delay, has been utilized—"

A chill of horror went through the Professor of Criminal Law. He had been very hot before, and now he was suddenly cold and shaken, like a person with a malarial chill. During the past several days he had heard that whoever came before the Governor with a plea for mercy or a plea for a delay in the date of execution, was met with a parrot-like recitation of the Governor's official decision to proceed with the execution, which he had made public a few weeks before now, on the third of August, and which he had apparently memorized. When he first heard these stories, the Professor of Criminal Law found them beyond normal belief; he dismissed them as the sort of nasty gossip and

143

malicious slander that was bound to be added to all the real sins attributable to the Governor. But here and now he was experiencing the thing himself. He was listening to the Governor of Massachusetts recite from memory a part of his own official decision; and the ordeal of listening to this became one of the most frightening and terrible experiences he had ever had. The moment he realized that the Governor was quoting his own decision, the whole atmosphere of the place seemed to change; the real world shimmered into the unsteady pattern of complete nightmare, and instead of a sturdy if reactionary leader of a mighty Commonwealth, he saw sitting before him a vessel both enigmatic and empty, the human form of which only made the situation more bizarre. It was only with an extreme effort of his will that the Professor was able to collect his thoughts and continue his argument.

"Forgive me, please, your Excellency," he said. "I feel it is not fair to pre-judge what we bring to you. I asked myself before coming here, whether I would approach you with a plea for mercy or a plea for justice. With some doubts remaining in my mind, I made a decision that I would not ask for mercy—"

"I realized at the outset," the Governor interrupted him, "that there were many sober minded and conscientious men and women who were genuinely troubled about the guilt or innocence of the men accused, and the fairness of their trial. It seemed to me—"

The insane horror continued to build as the Professor of Criminal Law realized once again that the Governor was quoting from his decision. His heart sank, and he fought against a wave of sickness, a mounting desire to vomit, the

144

culmination of heat, cold, and insanity; he resisted this nausea desperately while he waited for the Governor to finish. When the Governor at last finished quoting, the Professor continued his argument, although he doubted that the Governor was listening to him, or, if listening, had any logical comprehension of what he was saying. The Professor of Criminal Law continued his thesis that he had come there to plead for justice and not for mercy. He enumerated, slowly and meticulously, the roll-call of the most important witnesses who had spoken for Sacco and Vanzetti, pointing out that in all, there were over one hundred witnesses. He repeated some of the statements of those who had sworn under oath that neither Sacco nor Vanzetti could possibly have been at the scene of the crimes of which they were accused. He broke down the stories of the prosecution witnesses. He did not take long, for he had the whole of it at his fingertips, and less than fifteen minutes were needed to make a concise, incontestable, and concrete picture of innocence. Completing this analysis of the evidence, the Professor of Criminal Law said,

"The most bitter irony of it, your Excellency, is that Vanzetti has never in his life been to South Braintree. What a sorrowful thing that is to contemplate—that if he perishes tonight, he will die without ever having laid eyes upon the so-called scene of his crime."

The Governor waited politely now to see whether the Professor of Criminal Law had finished. When he saw that he had, the Governor said, very evenly and unemotionally, "It has been a difficult task to look back six years through other people's eyes. Many of the witnesses told me their story in a way I felt was more a matter of repetition than the product of their memory. Some witnesses replied that during the six years, they had forgotten incidents, and therefore could not remember. You see, it was a disagreeable experience, and for that very reason they have tried to forget it."

The Governor stopped speaking, and looked inquiringly at the Professor of Criminal Law and at the Writer. The Professor of Criminal Law felt cold, sick and listless, for once again, the Governor had quoted from the memorized decision; and the Professor of Criminal Law found himself unable to continue speaking, but turned to the Writer and looked at him pleadingly, wondering whether he too had recognized the source of the Governor's thoughtful and controlled eloquence.

"I, however, would ask for mercy," the Writer said simply. "I would ask for Christian mercy—in the memory of Christ who suffered."

"This is not a question for mercy," the Governor answered calmly. "The South Braintree crime was particularly brutal. The murder of the paymaster and the guard was not necessary to the robbery. It is wrong to ask for mercy. These men have had their day in court. Various delays have dragged this case through the courts for six years. I think these delays are inexcusable. I have no reason to delay it any further."

"My friend here beside me," the Writer said, his deep voice resonant but muted, "offered logic as reason for postponement. I ask for Christian mercy. Punishment has its dubious validity only in relation to the crime. I would be deceiving you, your Excellency, if I did not say that I myself believe these men are guilty of no crime except their radical beliefs; but even considering that they were guilty, have they not paid sufficiently? God's precious gift to man was for him to die once, never knowing the time of his going. But for seven years, these two poor men have died again and again. A thousand times, they have gone to their death before today, and what today has been to them, I cannot describe nor can anyone. Doesn't this touch you, your Excellency? My friend here beside me—both of us are proud people, but we come to you to beg as humbly as if we were slaves offering our lives and our human dignity to our master. We beg for the lives of these two men."

The Governor spoke one word now. He asked, "Why?" Suddenly he was earnest; and the one word encompassed all his powers of understanding. He wanted to know why— why did they come before him pleading for the lives of Sacco and Vanzetti? Why did anyone come before him? His manner implied that he would be grateful indeed if either of these two men could explain to him why they thought that Sacco and Vanzetti must not die.

Now the New York Writer shared the horror of the Professor of Criminal Law. The simple yet awful question, the one word directed at them by the Governor, made them speechless, and they could only wait silently for what might follow. The Governor also waited. The air in the room became heavy and motionless; life went out of the air. A grandfather clock in one corner ticked loudly and demandingly, but still all three of the men remained silent, and waited. What would have come of this, it is hard to say, for when the painful tension was near the breaking point, the door opened and the Governor's secretary said that Mrs. Sacco and Miss Vanzetti—Luigia Vanzetti, her name was, and she was Vanzetti's sister who had come all the great distance from Italy to plead for his life—stood outside, and were ready to see him if he would see them. Now the Governor turned to the Writer and the Professor of Criminal Law with incomprehensible and gentle apology. After all, they had come late for their appointment. He was so terribly sorry, but these two women had an appointment with him, and there were other appointments, and he had to be on schedule today. Did they want to go, or did they want to remain here and listen while he spoke to Miss Vanzetti and Mrs. Sacco?

The Professor of Criminal Law would have gone gladly, but the Writer answered for both of them, and said please, they would remain if the Governor did not mind.

No, he did not mind, the Governor said pleasantly, and then invited them to sit down on the claw-footed chairs that were ranged against the wall; thus they would be more comfortable. The Governor said that the best thing to do on a hot and trying day like this, was to make one's self as comfortable as one possibly could. He was now a considerate and thoughtful host, but the Professor of Criminal Law understood that this phase of him, like his reciting his own decision, was a choreography learned and practiced, a ritual that had no relationship to actual human concern. They sat down, and the door opened and the secretary led two women and a man into the Governor's office. The man was evidently a friend of the two women, as well as an interpreter for Miss Vanzetti, who spoke no English. She was a little woman, frail beyond belief, and both the Professor and the Writer looked at her with great curiosity. Until this moment, Sacco and Vanzetti had been two disembodied names. The sudden appearance of these two women had served to materialize both of the men before their eyes. The Writer was very much moved. He had heard that Mrs. Sacco was a beautiful woman, but he had not been prepared for the heartbreaking quality of her beauty; for this was a beauty that did not acknowledge itself. She was a woman without desire to be attractive to any man in the whole world but the one man who was denied to her; yet this very selflessness gave her the appearance of a Madonna out of some old and perfect Renaissance painting, a moment of womanhood caught by Raphael or Leonardo. Her beauty defied all the cheap and petty cliches that were a part of the culture of this land, and invented to impugn womanhood, not to ennoble it; and looking at her, the Writer wondered that he had ever thought of any other woman as being beautiful. Then he shook himself free of such feeling, for he felt in some way that it was unjust to the frightened and grief-stricken woman who stood before the Governor. Her grief was personal and very different from the strange and silent accusation of Vanzetti's sister.

There were no preliminaries to what Nicola Sacco's wife said. The words poured out of her like the soft running of a mountain brook. "I know you, Governor," she whispered. "I know that you have children. I know that you have a wife. And what do you think of when you look at your wife and children? Do you ever look at them, Governor, and think, good-by, good-by and farewell forever, and you will never see me again and I will never see you again?

149

Do you ever think of such things? My husband loves me better than he loves himself. How can I tell you what kind of a man he is? Nicola Sacco is gentle. What shall I say to you, Governor? If an ant comes into the house, then you step on it and kill it. An ant is an insect, and a man thinks nothing of an ant. But Nicola Sacco would pick up an ant and place it outside on the ground, and when I laughed at him, do you know what he would say to me? He would say, it has life, and therefore I must honor it. Life is precious. Think of those words, Governor. I want to try to make you see him the way he was with his children— never harsh, never angry, never impatient, never too busy. His ten fingers were slaves for them. What did the children want? Should he become a donkey and ride them on his back? Then he did. A troubadour to sing songs to them? That he also was. A fast runner to run races with them? That, too. And God help us if they should be sick—he was a nurse, and never left their bedside. Did I say *their* bedside? You see how the years catch up with me. I should have said *his* bedside, only the bedside of our little boy, Dante, for he never knew the little girl, who grew up while he lay in prison.

"Look at me, Governor. Am I the sort of woman who would be married to a murderer? Am I telling you about a man who kills in cold blood? Why will you destroy him? What terrible devils need to be satisfied with a burnt offering? What else can I say to you? I tried to think of everything I would say to you, and now it all comes down to nothing else but a man who is so full of love and kindness and good sweetness that he walked in his own garden like

Saint Francis. Do you know what he wanted? He wanted for the whole world to have the little bit that he had, a good wife and good children and a plain job where he could work each day and earn his daily bread. This is all that he wanted. This is why he was a radical. He said the people of the whole world should have his own happiness. But kill? He never, never killed. He never raised his hand to another man. Never. And now will you spare him, please, please? I will get down on my knees and kiss your feet, but spare him for his children and for me."

The Governor listened to all this without a shadow of emotion disturbing the small, neat, complacent features and folds of his clean-shaven face. He listened very politely and considerately, nor did he protest when Vanzetti's sister burst into a flood of Italian. The man who stood behind her translated without the emotional pitch that her voice contained; but in the very words there was a compelling and eloquent power. She told him how she had gone through France, and how the workers had persuaded her to lead a parade of tens of thousands of men and women through the streets of Paris.

"They said to me, good heart and good cheer, for you will go before the Governor of the land and tell him the truth about Bartolomeo Vanzetti, who is such a good man, a man of justice and clear thought and great dignity. Did I come here alone to tell you this? My father sent me. My father is an old, old man. He is as old as one of those old men in the Bible, and he said to me, go into the land of Egypt where my son is held prisoner. Go before the mighty of the land—and plead for my son's life."

It came as a shock to the Professor of Criminal Law to realize that the Writer was weeping. The Writer from New York wept simply and unashamedly, and then, deliberately, he dried his eyes and stared at the Governor. The Governor met his eyes, and that in no way disconcerted the leader of the Commonwealth. He had listened to all the two women had to say, and as before, when the Professor had spoken, he waited politely, to make quite certain that they had finished speaking. When he was sure of this he said, unemotionally and simply,

"I am terribly sorry that I cannot do something to alleviate your distress. I understand the source of your distress, but you see, the law is implacable under these circumstances. It has been a difficult task to look back six years through other people's eyes. Many of the witnesses told me their story in a way I felt was more a matter of repetition than a product of their memory—"

The Professor of Criminal Law could endure no more of this. "I must go," he said to the Writer. "Do you understand? I must go!" The Writer nodded. They rose and went out very quickly. Outside in the corridor, the reporters were waiting.

"Did he grant a stay?" one of them cried.

The Professor of Criminal Law shook his head. He and the Writer walked on outside into the sunshine where the picket line still moved. The Writer turned to his companion and shook hands with him.

"Well," the Writer said, "this is the world we live in. There is no other that I can be sure of. I am glad to have met you. I will remember having met you, and your courage."

152

"I have no courage," the Professor of Criminal Law answered plaintively.

Then the Writer went back to the picket line, all he could do now, and began to walk again, and the Professor of Criminal Law moved with heavy steps toward the offices of the Defense Committee.

Chapter 11

EVEN BEFORE four o'clock on August 22nd, there were people at Union Square in New York City, hundreds of people, some of them standing quietly in little groups, some of them walking about slowly, and still others moving as if they were looking for something not easily found; and the police were there too. On the rooftops around the square, police had set up observation posts and machine gun nests, and the people in the square, looking up, could see the figures of the police silhouetted against the sky, and the blunt, ugly gun muzzles pointing down at them. People looking up wondered, "Well, now, what do they expect?" Already, there was a thematic silence in the place; did they expect that out of here, out of Union Square in New York City, an army would begin to march to Boston to free Sacco and Vanzetti?

And even if the police thought of anything as crazy as that, they should have realized that it was too late. It was Monday afternoon already. Even a man's heart would have to fly quickly to reach Boston before midnight.

154

It was shortly after four o'clock that the square began to fill. Strangely, women came first, many of them; no one understood why that should be. They were mothers and housewives, plain working class women for the most part, poorly dressed, with the dry, hard hands used for the whole sustenance of life. A good many of them had their children with them, some two or three little children whom they led by hand, some smaller children carried in arm—and the children knew that there was no pleasure out of this particular pilgrimage. When the women arrived, two small, informal meetings began, with the speakers standing on boxes, but the police moved in quickly and dispersed those meetings.

At a little after four o'clock, large groups of workers began to arrive in the square. Already in the square were hundreds of fur and hat workers who had laid down their tools for this day in protest and sympathy, and now there moved among them, mixing with them, Italian laborers who had gone on the job at seven in the morning and left it at four in the afternoon. Straight from work they came to Union Square, carrying their lunch pails, hot and tired and dirty with the day's labor. They came in groups of four and seven and ten, off this job and that job, and at half past four, a meeting began among them. The police moved toward this meeting, but other workers also moved toward it; and it suddenly became too big and the police left it alone.

A group of merchant seamen came into the square, Irish and Poles and Italians, half a dozen black men and two Chinese, and they kept together as they moved through the thickening eddies of people. They came to

155

where two women stood weeping, and then they halted in a sort of embarrassed and impotent respect. Not far from them, an evangelist fell upon his knees and cried out, "Brethren and sisteren, let us pray!" A few people gathered about him, but not many. Then up to the square, around Broadway from Fourteenth Street, came a cavalcade of three long, open police cars, carrying the big brass from the Center Street station. They got out and looked at the square. Then they put their heads together and had a meeting of sorts; then they drove their cars into West Seventeenth Street, where they formed an off-limits command post. A dozen policemen guarded the cars, which were loaded with riot guns and tear gas grenades.

The policemen on the rooftops watched with interest as the square filled up. At first, looking down, they saw individual men and women standing here and there; the changes which followed seemed, from high above, mechanical in nature and as inevitable in process as a chemical transformation would be. Suddenly individuals were grouped; no signal was given, no one was seen to move; it happened in silence—and in the same silence, the clumps of men and women fell together into three or four masses. All around the square were clothing factories; by five o'clock the workers poured out of them onto the street, and almost in minutes Union Square had been turned into a connected sea of people—and yet it had only begun. The ladies garment workers walked from uptown; the furniture and paper workers pressed into the square from downtown below Fourteenth Street, and from the publishing houses and printing places on Fourth Avenue, other streams flowed toward the square. Hundreds became

156

thousands, and the restless, searching movement of people halted. Now it became a mass of mankind. And a noise went up from it, a muted, wordless, inchoate noise that began like a whisper of angry prayer.

Any one of the policemen upon the rooftops would have been insensitive indeed not to have felt a certain awe at the manner in which so many thousands of people had come together, not to have wondered—at least a little—what force two poor, condemned men could exert to call out such love and concern. Yet even if they wondered about this, the whole world stood between them and the people below, the connection being derivable only from the bandoleers of machine gun bullets that lay heaped here and there. The policemen were for the most part church-going men, but it did not occur to any one of them, as it did to an Episcopalian minister down below among the people, that when Christ was taken by the soldiers of Pilate, then somewhere in the city of Jerusalem, the plain working people had come together like this, to hope and pray that out of their unity and strength, something would come.

The Episcopalian minister had never before in all his life been to anything like this, never to a demonstration of working people, never to a mass protest meeting. He had never walked on a picket line or felt the impact of a wave of horse-mounted police swinging their long riot sticks, or heard the chatter of a machine gun searching haphazardly for people's lives, or felt the stinging pain in his eyes of tear gas, or covered his head with his hands to save his skull from the pounding clubs of hate-maddened police. His life had been a very sheltered life, but in that way it was not greatly different from the lives of thousands of middle class Americans—yet this thing had reached him, too. Like so many others in America, he had gone out of himself and joined with the suffering of millions, through the two condemned men in Massachusetts, and day by day, his understanding of what was happening in Massachusetts deepened. Today, unable to bear the thought of being alone, unable to endure the waiting, he had walked downtown to Union Square—where he found so many companions to walk the hill of Calvary together with him.

Now he felt not less sadness, but more peace. He moved through the crowd. Some looked at him curiously, he was so different from them, in his clerical dress, with his pale, thin features, his graying hair, and his almost delicate manner of motion; but he did not mind this, nor was he disturbed by their stares. It surprised him somewhat that he could feel so much at ease among them, and it also terrified him a little that he, thinking of himself as a man of God, had already spent almost three-score of years in places where these people never came. How that could have been, he did not really understand—but he would, in time.

He looked at the people around him and guessed at what they did to earn their daily bread. Once when he stumbled, a Negro with a sleeveless leather jacket smelling of paint and varnish, helped him to his feet. He saw a carpenter with all his tools, and a woman who wore a crucifix touched his arm tenderly as he moved past. A group of women wept quitely and they spoke to each other in a tongue foreign to him. He heard many tongues spoken here, and wondered again at the strange and varied quality of these people, about whom he knew so little.

Then someone stopped him and asked him would he lead a prayer. That was the last thing that had been on his mind when he turned his steps to Union Square, but how could he refuse prayer? Full of fear and trepidation, he nevertheless nodded and said he would. He pointed out that he was an Episcopalian, as perhaps few of these folks here were, but nevertheless, he would lead the prayer if that was asked of him.

"It doesn't matter," they said. "Prayer is prayer."

His arm was taken, and he was led through the crowd, and then he was helped onto a platform from where he looked down upon an apparently endless sea of faces.

"God help me," he said to himself. "Help me now. I have no prayers for this. Never was I in a church like this, and never did I see such people before. What will I say to them?"

Nor did he really know until he began to speak. Then he found himself saying, ". . . whatever our strength is, take from it and give it to the two humble and good men in Charlestown Prison, so that they may live and mankind may be redeemed. . . ." But when he had finished, he knew it was wrong; from a person of faith, he had become a man of fear and questioning, nor would he ever again be as he was before. . . .

And still the square filled. Clerks and street car conductors and weary-eyed dress finishers and bakers and operators and mechanics—they moved into Union Square in a silent procession, apparently without end. Many left, but many more came and took their places, and the great sea of humanity seemed to exist motionless and unchanged.

Word of it went to Boston. The New York Defense Committee for Sacco and Vanzetti was only a few blocks from Union Square. The people who worked there had worked for days without sleep or rest, and now, in their agonizing weariness, they took excitement and comfort from the masses of people in the square, and sent word of it to Boston. "Tens of thousands," they cried over the telephone, "are pouring into Union Square. There never has been a protest like this. Surely it will be understood there."

They were not alone in thinking that there had never been such a protest as this. Through a window that overlooked one part of Union Square, a man had watched the people come, and he too had the strange feeling that he was witnessing something new and terrible and wonderful— something never quite equaled before in all the mighty demonstrations of American working people. This man was able to watch the square from his own office, and he had spent the afternoon in his office waiting for a number of others who were to come and meet with him. Like himself, they were trade unionists. He was at the window looking down at Union Square at half past three, when the first one of the group scheduled to meet in his office that day, a leader in the organized needle trades in the city, joined him.

The man at the window—whom we can call the Chairman—turned around, smiled with immediate pleasure, and offered him his hand. They were old friends. Since his childhood, the Chairman had worked in his own industry, first at the most menial type of work as floorboy and delivery boy, and then as an operater and cutter as he learned the trade. Now he was a leader in his union, a man of growing influence and importance in organized labor in the city of New York. He had a comfortable office and he could look forward to a pay check more often than not. In spite of these fortunate circumstances that had come so lately, he remained very much as his friends had known him, simple, direct, and filled with eager and unabating enthusiasm. He was not tall, but gave the impression of height, and was solidly built, with a square and pleasant face; and in the warmth of his movements and the directness of his gestures, there was something so amazingly simple that most people found it quite irresistible. Now the Chairman took the needle trades leader by the shoulders and steered him to the window, pointing out over the square.

"Look at that! Isn't it something to see!" he cried.

"Yes—I suppose so," the needle trades leader answered. "It's also August 22nd."

"That doesn't mean the fight is over."

"No? What then? What do we do with a few hours left?"

"Delay the execution somehow. Get twenty-four hours—that's enough. With that much time, we make our plea again to the Federation leaders. There's only one thing that will save Sacco and Vanzetti, but it will also save us—and the American labor movement."

"And what is that?"

"A general strike."

"You are dreaming," the needle trades leader said, almost angrily.

"Am I? Then this is one dream that will come true."

"And suppose there is no delay in the execution?"

"There must be," the Chairman insisted.

"I would not talk to the others about a general strike—because it's a dream. It can't be done, and if we should call for it, we cut ourselves off."

"Then you would let them die?"

"Am I killing them? But our dreams won't save them." He pointed to Union Square. "There we are—all that we can do now. Pick up the phone and plead with the Governor of Massachusetts, but don't dream about general strikes. The men who can make such things have sold out, five times over, sold themselves and their workers, and the unions that would lead a general strike have been smashed and washed clean in blood. Don't dream any more."

"I'll still dream," the Chairman answered, and with that he fell silent, apparently immersed in his own thoughts.

For a while now the two of them stood watching the demonstration below in wordless attention. Presently they were joined by a rank and file leader of the Italian construction workers in the city. A steel worker who had been fighting ten years to organize the union in Gary, Indiana, and who had come into the city only this morning, also joined them, as did two copper miners from Montana. The two copper miners had arrived in New York a couple of hours before. They were both fairly young men, with dry skin and long, hard faces, pocked all over with cinder specks. All the distance from Butte they had come by rail, riding in box cars, in gondola cars, and sometimes on the rods underneath the cars; and in this fashion they beat their way into New York, perhaps not completely on schedule, but not too long after they had promised the Chairman that they would be there. They shook hands with him warmly,

162

studying him all the while with frank curiosity, for they had heard much of him, yet had never seen him before. The Chairman, however, knew them well by reputation, and knew the story of how for five years they had been trying to organize the copper and silver miners of the mountain states. They had learned in a hard school, and had emerged from it, as needs be, hard men.

As time went on, still other trade union leaders joined the group, and by now there were more than twelve people seated in the office of the Chairman. A shoe worker was there, a Negro from the Railroad Brotherhood, and another Negro from the laundry workers' union. There were people from the jewelry workers, the hat makers, and bakers—altogether, as the Chairman thought, as good and representative a group of trade unionists as one could hope to bring together on such very short notice on this August 22nd of 1927.

The Chairman called the meeting to order, but even while he spoke, he could not keep his eyes from turning toward the window. His words were as restless as his motions, and he paced back and forth uneasily, referring again and again to the lateness of the hour.

"So it would seem," he said, "that we should have met a week or a month ago—as some of us did, and we did whatever we could do." He struggled with the language. His voice had an accent out of another place and time—but the others in the room also had the mark of their wandering and seeking on their tongues.

"Anyway, today here we are," the Chairman said. "And as far as I can see, it is the last day. That's the way it is with these things. It doesn't seem possible that there can

163

be a finish, but the finish comes and there we are. All morning I was thinking of what we can do, and still I'm not sure. Our people are out, and most of them are down there in Union Square. In the same way, many of the dress makers and cloak makers are out—but it won't be enough or change anything. So I lay awake all last night thinking about what we could do."

"What can we do?" the steel worker asked. "There are a few hours left. You can't turn the world over in a few hours. It's not like we had a movement like they have in some places in Europe. In steel, our heads have been beaten until they're bloody, and we talk in whispers. What can we do now?"

"Maybe you been whispering too long," the man from the bakers' union answered. "Jesus Christ! Will there never come an end to the way we walk around with our heads down, whispering?"

"Maybe," the Chairman said, "if we think of it in a certain way. I keep asking myself why these two men go to die tonight. So what can I answer myself except one thing—they die for us, for you and me, for fur workers, needle workers and steel workers. I put it plain and straight-forward. The bosses are afraid—not of you and me. I wish to God they were afraid of you and me! No, not that. They are afraid of what they see moving and stirring and turn-ing over everywhere in the world. They are afraid of what the people did in Russia. A red sound comes out of Russia, and they don't like that sound. So this time they made their demonstration to us. They are saying to us, we have Sacco and Vanzetti, and you—you who talk so much about organized labor and the strength of organized labor,

164

you can scream and shout and protest and squirm and cry and whimper, and not one God-damned bit of good is it going to do. Yell as you please! Tonight Sacco and Vanzetti will die, and a lesson will be driven home. Plain. Unvarnished. That's how I see it."

"That's the way it is," one of the copper miners said. "Brothers, that's the way it has always been. They take off their gloves and they show it to us plain."

The Italian, who was one of a group trying to organize the construction workers, and who had suffered a fractured skull two months before because he would not be bought off, seemed about to say something; but when the Chairman nodded at him, he shook his head and remained silent. The leader from the needle trades said slowly and carefully,

"Brothers, today is a lesson in the expensive luxury of talk. We have fallen into a habit of talking, and now each minute we talk away has no replacement. We come to the end, and I think we must do something. I don't know how. I don't know what. I look to you to tell me. We have brothers here who came from far, far places of the country, where there are millions of workers like themselves. How do these workers feel about Sacco and Vanzetti, and what will they do?"

"What can they do now?" the steel worker wanted to know. "It's easy to talk about the workers and what the workers should know. But the worker has had his head beaten in and his belly shrunken, and then he reads in the paper that he is a Russian spy if he opens his yap. We called out our people two weeks ago, and some of them went out and some of them didn't. But those who laid down their tools and struck for Sacco and Vanzetti paid a price, and today they are sitting, many of them, and looking at their wives and listening to what a kid sounds like when he is hungry. And tonight Sacco and Vanzetti are going to die. How many hours are left? If we had unions, great, powerful organizations like they got in France, we could move in with them, but we haven't got that and there's no use fooling ourselves. And where the Federation has got a good union and a strong union, they laugh at us and say that these God-damned Italians deserve what's coming to them. So there it is."

One of the copper miners asked desperately, hungrily, "What about the longshoremen here in New York? If they would go off even now, it might help a little bit. Anyway, it is too quiet here. The city is standing still. Even down there in the square the people are standing still. Nothing is going to happen while they are standing still. You can pull out a half-million workers, but until they start to march, the world won't turn over. I can't understand it. Why are they standing still like that? Can't you get them marching? You talked about these two men going to die tonight for us. I would put it a little more flatly, my friends. I don't know this city. I don't know how it is here. But out where we are, we see it plain and clear. So it was our decision to drop everything and head into New York, and maybe argue and plead and stand up and say this is the way it's got to be. You can't stand still when you can count the hours and the minutes that are left."

"I have counted them," the Chairman said sadly. "I feel the way you do, my friend. We got a little experience in how to struggle ourselves here, but we don't know how to walk down there and start ten thousand people marching. They have to want to march, and there has to be a situation which tells them that when they begin to march, those machine guns on top of the buildings all around the square won't open up and chew them up. You learn slow, so slow it's enough to make you want to put your head down and cry, but you learn a little, and it does no good to scream that something you can't stop must be stopped. I think maybe we can do something, but only if the execution is delayed."

Now the Italian spoke. He agreed that no one knew whether much could be done in the little time that was left. Like the Chairman, he spoke slowly, organizing his words and his thoughts out of another tongue and another culture. Of course, he said, they would do what they could do, send telegrams to the Governor of Massachusetts and to the President of the United States, use the telephone where the telephone might be effective, and even now, go to the workers in the few hours that were left. "But," he went on, "suppose everything we try, it fails, and then Sacco and Vanzetti die? My heart will hurt, I think. Maybe not so much as the suffering of Sacco's wife, of his children, but still you can be sure I suffer. Then is it the end of the world? Do they die for nothing? Is it defeat, and we are smashed down, and spit on us for nothing, for no reason? No. I say the fight goes on, and maybe we meet again tomorrow, and we will talk about this tomorrow, and if the men are dead, then we will make a warm spot among us for their memory. This I say. Yes?"

The others looked at him. There was a small work-worn woman from the needle trades, and as she looked at him, her pale blue eyes filled with tears, and the tears trickled down her cheeks.

"You are right, brother," she said. "You are right."

They sat for a while in silence, and then the two representatives of the copper miners got up and walked to the window and looked down at Union Square. A great mass of people now filled the square, and the two copper miners watched them in the manner of a silent salute. As they watched, they listened to the recommendation of the Chairman that all of them join together immediately in calling for a general strike of city workers, a protest nationally and a great march from Union Square to City Hall, providing the execution could be delayed. So it was put into words, their plans, their dreams and their hopes. To some extent it excluded their own strength, and the two copper miners were tired with all the long distance they had come and all the struggles behind them in which they had been beaten back and smashed down. Yet as they stood there and watched the mass of people in Union Square, strength and comfort seemed to flow back into them, and they began to see a glimmer of hope in the course of action the Chairman was spelling out. It was their own strength and the strength of others like them that was flowing back into their veins. And now, in their thoughts at least, they imagined a stirring, a motion in the great mass of people, a movement which, if executed and completed, would be irresistible.

Chapter 12

AT FIVE O'CLOCK, the Judge demanded fretfully of his wife, "Well, isn't he here yet? I don't know why he isn't here. He said that he would be here by five o'clock."

"I don't know why you should be so upset about it," she answered him. "Just suppose he is a few minutes late—any number of things could have delayed him."

"That's just it. When we need him, any number of things can delay him When we don't need him, he's here. Nothing delays him then. Oh yes, you can be sure of that; if there's no need of him, then he is here."

"Of course this is a most trying day," she said. "And it's so hot here! Why don't you go out on the porch? Then you will see him as soon as he comes. He's sure to be here any moment now."

The Judge thought that he would. It was an excellent idea, because it would be cool and pleasant out on the porch. His wife said she would bring some cold lemonade out, and some of her nut cookies of which the Pastor was very fond; and then when the Pastor came, she would leave the two of them alone to chat with each other.

The Judge went out on the wide, old fashioned porch and seated himself in a wicker chair. The porch was cool and shaded and offered a maximum of privacy; for it was closed in with long blinds of split bamboo, which allowed a trickle of daylight and sunlight to seep through, but made it impossible for anyone outside to look in. The Judge leaned back in his wicker chair and attempted manfully to compose himself. Earlier on this same day, he had experienced an abrupt and sudden spasm of pain under his left breast—and his first thought has been, "Well, here it is finally, with all that I have been through and all that I have suffered." They had called the doctor immediately, and the doctor came and examined him very carefully and reassured him that it was no more than a little gas, the result of something he had eaten for breakfast which did not agree with him.

Then he had said to the doctor, "Well, you know what kind of a day this is going to be."

"A very trying day, I should imagine," the doctor had replied.

"Most trying, most trying," the Judge said. "I am no longer a young man. You see now the rewards thrown to virtue, like a dry bone to an old dog. You should be grateful that you are a physician and not a jurist."

"Each to his own trade," the doctor had answered. "Mine is not without its problems."

"Now, sitting in the wicker chair, the Judge reflected with some relief that the best part of the day had already passed by, and that in only a few hours more, August 22nd would be over. When all was said and done, he was calmer about this difficult period than most people would have been. Of course it helped to have the two policemen stationed out front at the entrance to his place; but the upsetting threats which he had faced today were psychological rather than physical. The several hundred letters that had come in the morning mail were more of a menace to his peace of mind than to his physical welfare. He had only read a handful of these letters, yet he noted with a certain amount of self-justification the remarkable similarity of each to the others. They might have been written by a group of consultants, if you considered the uniformity of the manner in which they denounced him and pleaded for the lives of these two incredible men. Of more concern than letters, were some of the periodicals that had anonymously been sent to him. A periodical with an article about the case, which contained a reference to him, would be opened and refolded, so that the reference was on the outside. Invariably, this reference would be encircled by a heavy crayon line, or perhaps a stubby, garish red arrow would be drawn on the page, pointing to the reference. One such periodical with both the circle and the red arrow, printed on what the Judge commonly referred to as "butcher store paper," had arrived that morning and had captured his attention to a point where, in spite of himself, he read on, fascinated, until he had completed the entire passage. It read as follows:

"One cannot help but wonder how the Judge will pass the day of August 22nd. Will he celebrate? Will he invite in a few of his very best and closest friends, open a bottle of old New England port brought over to this sacred soil a hundred years before, and drink a benevolent toast to the death of a shoemaker and a fish peddler? Or will the Judge spend the day alone in quiet contemplation of the singular rewards for a man who does his duty as he sees it and as his conscience leads him to it? Or perhaps the Judge will continue in his hour-to-hour routine, armed with the stern righteousness of an upright man, and admitting in no way that this day is different from any other.

"Howsoever the Judge decides, we do not envy him. It was well spoken by the poet who said, *The paths of glory lead but to the grave.* Howsoever he chooses to pass the day of Monday, August 22nd, the Judge will be constantly aware that he, like all other men and women, is mortal. Somewhere in back of his mind, there will ring that solemn reminder, *Judge not, lest ye be judged.*"

Having read this, the Judge was at first not so much upset as disconcerted, and he ruffled through the magazine angrily, eager to see which red, communist, radical, socialist or anarchist journal had taken this irritating tack. To his amazement, he discovered that the passage he had just perused, had been printed in the national journal of a Protestant sect, one closely allied to his own. Somehow or other, this discovery was so disturbing and so very annoying that it fixed itself in his mind, and plagued him and troubled him until he could no longer endure it. That was when he phoned his own local pastor and asked him whether the Pastor could visit and spend a little time with him. The Pastor, having a busy day, asked whether it would not be all right to postpone the visit until late in the afternoon. The Judge agreed that the Pastor should come at five o'clock and remain to dinner with them. This

172

was still in the forenoon, and the Judge did not think that the remaining hours would impose any new difficulties upon him which he could not engage and surmount himself.

The actuality of the afternoon was somewhat different from what he had anticipated. Life did not leave the Judge alone today, and all day long there was a succession of messages, telegrams, special delivery letters and phone calls. Clothe himself though he might in his own righteousness, the Judge was nevertheless distraught and shaken. Now, at five o'clock, he was a troubled man who needed urgently the counsel of a friend and a minister; whereupon, his relief at hearing a step on the walk outside can be understood, and it can also be understood why, when the Pastor stepped into the twilight of the porch, the Judge greeted him eagerly and more gratefully and enthusiastically perhaps than their past relationship warranted. However, the Pastor understood that this must be an unusual day in the Judge's life, and was thereby prepared to be most tolerant of any and all unusual if not unexpected actions which the old man might take.

The Judge shook hands warmly with the Pastor and invited him to sit in one of the big wicker chairs. The Pastor did so gratefully, placing his straw hat and his stick carefully on the low table which held a pile of newspapers and periodicals. When the maid came out, carrying a tray of glasses, lemonade and cookies, the Judge poured a glass of lemonade for each of them, and the Pastor wiped his brow and drank the cool liquid gratefully. Then the Pastor picked up one of the nut cookies, bit into it, and smiled with pleasure as he pronounced it excellent.

"And I do like your wife's lemonade," he said. "It tastes fresh—not like something she made last week and kept around. So many people make lemonade in the summer time, and so rarely does it have that fresh, good taste of the newly squeezed lemon. I have always held that lemons are a valuable repository of healthful humors—if one may be permitted a rather old fashioned expression. I believe that drinking lemonade is an excellent way to ward off distempers of the summer time. I have also heard that it is good for dropsy and for dizzy spells—"

Thus the Pastor chatted while he drank lemonade and munched cookies. He was measuring up to his reputation as a cheerful person who liked to look always at the best and brightest side of things. He made considerable contrast to the Judge's worried gauntness; for the Pastor was a roly-poly figure, with a little round pot-belly, and cheeks as plump and shiny as new apples.

For a while, the Judge listened to him patiently, but at last could endure the flow of senseless chatter no longer, and reminded the Pastor that he had desired to talk with him about certain fairly disturbing matters.

"Disturbing?" the Pastor queried, raising his brows. "I do think that right here at the beginning we should pause and inquire and perhaps set certain unhappy notions at rest. You, of all people, sir, have little reason to be disturbed. Judgment, like a ministership, must be considered as an extension of God's will. Without judgment, there is anarchy. Without ministerial tending, there is atheism. We are both shepherds, and in effect, our likenesses and callings rest upon opposite sides of the same coin. Would you not say so, sir?"

"I have never considered it in just that fashion," the Judge replied.

"Do so now. By all means, do so," the Pastor urged, sipping his lemonade.

The Judge said, "Nevertheless, you can understand my predicament. For seven years, this case has dragged on. I have become an old man since it began. My peace of mind has fled. Now, wherever I am, they point to me and whisper about me, and say, *Him? Oh, yes, he is the one who passed sentence on the anarchists.*"

"Yet isn't that obvious?" the Pastor said soothingly. "If not you, then another. But fate, as directed by the Almighty God, chose you. Someone had to sit in judgment, and you were chosen. It was not you, but the jury, who found them guilty, and once the jury had done this, then you were only carrying out your solemn and sworn duty by passing sentence upon them. There are people of gross materialism in this materialistic age," the Pastor added, helping himself to another cookie and nodding his thanks to the Judge who poured another glass of lemonade, "who will say that there is no judgment after yours. However, the final judgment is still to be rendered. There is another bar before which these two men must stand, and there is another who will sit in judgment and hear their arguments and pleas. You, sir, have done your duty. Can anyone do more than that?"

"It is very comforting to hear you say that. However, just look at this," and the Judge handed him the crayon-circled passage in the religious journal.

The Pastor read it and snorted with justifiable anger. "Ha!" he cried. "I would like to confront the man who wrote that. I would like to see and know some facts about him—just what sort of a Christian he is. That's what I would like to know. Judge not, he says, yet in the same breath he judges. I question both his calling and his holiness!"

"Then you don't think it can be regarded as any sort of an official position?"

"Official position? My word, no, not at all, sir."

"Do you know," the Judge said, "I have been sleeping badly, dreaming very bad dreams, some of them monstrous things. It is not a bad conscience, however. Such a thought I reject as absurd."

"You should reject it," the Pastor agreed, reaching toward the cookies again. "You do rightly."

"My conscience is clear. I have no regrets about what I have done. I examined the evidence and I weighed it very thoughtfully; but it went deeper than the simple problem of evidence. I tell you, Pastor, when I first looked at those two men, I knew that they were guilty. I could see it in the way they walked, in their manner of speech, in the way they stood before me. Guilt was written all over them. For seven years, their lawyers have entered motions and pleas and exceptions and arguments of every sort conceivable under the sun. Could anyone have listened to the arguments more patiently, heard the motions more patiently? Was there ever a motion which I refused to hear? But how could I alter my original concept?"

"If no evidence appeared to controvert it, then most certainly you could not."

Now the Judge leaped to his feet and began to pace back and forth on the porch. "Of course there is something else,"

176

he said with considerable agitation. "Do you know what I am thinking? Do you know how it seems to me? It seems to me that these two men welcome death, seek death for their own dark purposes. In the beginning, they had only one thought, one desire—to destroy, to overthrow, to set aside all that we have built up, and treasure and venerate. When I look about me at this old New England of ours, at its tree-shaded houses, its green lawns, and its clear-eyed, open-faced children, then I shudder at the thought of all this passing away by fire and torch. Something has happened here in this old land of ours. Alien people have come to it, slinking, scurvy, dark-skinned people, people afraid to look you straightforwardly in the eye. They come with their own language and live in hovels and cast a pall of darkness all over the land. How I hate them! Is it wrong for me to hate them this way?"

"I am afraid it is wrong to hate," the Pastor said, almost regretfully.

"I see your point of view." The Judge nodded, continuing his pacing. "But what does one say to communists and socialists and anarchists? Suppose they were in power in the courts? How much justice would there be for people like you or me, or for any of our people of the old stock? They would only have to hear a clear voice or face a straightforward pair of blue eyes, and they would launch into their own dance of death. They come here with their cursed agitation, with their leaflets and their pamphlets, sowing discontent, agitating, disturbing the plain working people, setting brother against brother, whispering everywhere, *More pay! More wages! Your employer is evil! Your employer is a devil! Why shouldn't what is his belong to*

177

you? Where there was peace and contentment before, there is only hatred and strife now. Where a garden bloomed before, they have made a desert. When I think that we could have here in this blessed New England of ours, the cursed ignorance and hatred, the slave camps and the famine and the forced labor of Russia, then my blood boils and my heart stops beating. Is it wrong, then, for me to hate those who violate my land, those who hate the name of America and the past of America?"

"It is never wrong to hate the servants of the devil," the Pastor said, grateful that he was able to bring comfort again "You can rest assured on that point. How else can we struggle with the Prince of Darkness?"

"I am not saying that I am without fault," the Judge cried, whirling suddenly to face the Pastor. "In some matters I acted foolishly and thoughtlessly. But must I pay for such small lapses for the rest of my life? It is quite true that I said something in irritation about what I did to those two anarchist bastards. Strong language, you will say, but I had some strong feelings at the moment it passed my lips, and I thought that I was saying it in the company of gentlemen. However, I found out that the case was very different, and that my listeners were hardly gentlemen. The next day my words were all over, everywhere, and now they claim that I acted on the basis of personal hatred and malevolence. Nothing could be further from the truth. I tell you, Pastor, nothing could be further from the truth. This case has taken an awful toll from me. I have given my very life blood to it. When will I know peace again?"

The Pastor nodded, hastily swallowing the cookie he

had been chewing. "One should never despair on that score. Time is the great healer—the great healer. All things but God Almighty succumb to time. We look around us today, enduring the great burden of our trials and tribulations of the moment, and we understandably say to ourselves that this will never pass and that there will never be any surcease from this. But that is a human point of view, and to err is human. God heals in his own way. Time is the staff of God. Time is a very great healer, sir, you can be sure of that."

"It is most comforting to hear you say that." The Judge ceased his pacing and reseated himself now in the big wicker chair. "Very comforting, indeed. So few people have any idea of what we have endured, myself, the District Attorney, the members of the jury, yes, and even many of the witnesses for the State. We have been accused of hating foreigners, of having biased feelings toward Italians. These people come to our countryside and lust through it and dirty it and rob and commit murder without restraint, and if we take exception to these deeds, we are told that we are filled with bias and prejudice and hatred. It has been a burden, believe me, Pastor. And of course every evil, subversive and un-American element in the whole nation has seized upon this case. They have used it to undermine authority and to hold people like myself and his Excellency, the Governor, in contempt. They even slander the venerable President of the University, whose inquiry into the case confirmed the very findings we made, and whose decision was that these men were justly sentenced."

179

"A brave man always pays a price," the Pastor nodded. "But you have this consolation, that you have done your duty uprightly and well."

The Pastor reached into his pocket, took out his fine, thin, gold watch, and peered at the face. "Dear me," he said.

"But you will stay for dinner?" the Judge protested.

"I am afraid not," the Pastor sighed. "I know that I did say something about it, but I must get back to my study and to work."

As a matter of fact, the Pastor was full of impatience now, for in the course of the conversation, the whole pattern of a sermon had come to his mind, and he felt that there was an obligation on his part to write down his thoughts before they fled. The Judge expressed his regrets, but repeated that his talk with the Pastor had been very consoling. He accompanied the Pastor to the gate, and then returned to the coolness of the porch.

Chapter 13

AFTER THE PASTOR HAD DEPARTED, the Judge settled himself in his wicker chair as comfortably as he could, and put his feet up on a footrest. In the hope of diverting his thoughts, he picked up a mystery novel and tried to read, but the light was too poor on the porch, and after he had read only a few lines, he dozed. If the truth be told, cumulative tensions of the day had wearied him greatly, and the release that the Pastor had given him allowed him to fall asleep easily and quickly. But while the act of falling asleep was quick and gentle, the sleep itself was short and restless. As had happened so often lately, he was disturbed by dreams, and more often than not, the dreams recreated situations of the past.

Now in his sleep, his thoughts go back to that day not so long ago, Saturday, the ninth of April, of this same year, when he had passed sentence upon the two anarchists. That was almost five months ago, but the incident was deeply engraved upon his memory, and once again in his half-sleep, he sits at the bench in the crowded courtroom, his papers spread out before him, ready to impose sentence for a crime committed seven long years ago, upon two men who had spent those seven long years in prison. How strangely he looks at them as they walk into the courtroom! And how strange they seem to him! He has almost forgotten who they are and what they look like. Somehow, after all these years, they seem neither so ragged nor so desperate as they were in his memory, even though they take their places in that peculiar and barbaric apparatus of New England justice, the cage where prisoners sit when they are tried or sentenced.

The Judge taps with his gavel, and the District Attorney rises and says,

"May it please the Court, the matter under consideration at this session is indictments Nos. 5545 and 5546, Commonwealth vs. Nicola Sacco and Bartolomeo Vanzetti.

"It appears by the record of this Court, if your Honor please, that on indictment No. 5545, Commonwealth vs. Nicola Sacco and Bartolomeo Vanzetti, that these defendants stand convicted of murder in the first degree. The records are clear at the present time, and I therefore move the Court for the imposition of sentence. The statute allows the Court some discretion as to the time within which this sentence may be imposed. Having in mind, and at the request of the defendants' counsel, to which the Commonwealth readily assents, I would suggest that the sentence to be imposed shall be executed some time during the week beginning Sunday, July 10 next."

The Judge nods to show that he is in general agreement with the District Attorney. The clerk of the court turns to the first of the two condemned men and says,

"Nicola Sacco, have you anything to say why sentence of death should not be passed upon you?"

Sacco rises. He looks directly at the Judge for a long moment before he speaks; and in spite of himself, the Judge is constrained to drop his eyes. Sacco begins to speak in a very soft voice. As he continues to speak, his voice strengthens, but the pitch does not rise. He is almost detached from the whole scene as he says,

"Yes sir. I am not an orator. It is not very familiar with me the English language, and as I know, as my friend has told me, my comrade Vanzetti will speak more long, so I thought to give him the chance.

"I never know, never heard, even read in history anything so cruel as this Court. After seven years prosecuting they still consider us guilty. And these gentle people here are arrayed with us in this Court today.

"I know the sentence will be between two class, the oppressed class and the rich class. We fraternize the people with the books, with the literature. You persecute the people, tyrannize over them and kill them. We try the education of people always. You try to put a path between us and some other nationality that hates each other. That is why I am here today on this bench, for having been the oppressed class. Well, you are the oppressor.

"You know it Judge—you know all my life, you know why I have been here, and after seven years that you have been persecuting me and my poor wife, and you still today sentence us to death. I would like to tell all my life, but what is the use? You know all about what I say before, and my friend—that is, my comrade—will be talking, because he is more familiar with the language, and I will give him a chance. My comrade, the kind man to all the children. You forget all the population that has been with us for seven years, to sympathize and give us all their energy and all their kindness. You do not care for them. Among peoples and the comrades and the working class there is a big legion of intellectual people which have been with us for seven years, but still the Court goes ahead. And I think I thank you all, you peoples, my comrades who have been with me for seven years, with the Sacco-Vanzetti case, and I will give my friend Vanzetti a chance to speak.

"I forgot one thing which my comrade remember me. As I said before, the Judge knows all my life, and he know that I never been guilty, never—not yesterday nor today nor forever."

He finishes, and a terrible hush settles over the court. In his dream of it, it seems to the Judge that the hush lasts for an eternity, but actually it is no more than seconds. The clerk interrupts it. Precise and business like, he rises to his feet, points to the second condemned man, and demands,

"Bartolomeo Vanzetti, have you anything to say why sentence of death should not be passed on you?"

A bridge of silence connects this brutal question with Vanzetti's answer. When he first rises to his feet, he says nothing, but instead looks about the courtroom, at the Judge, at the District Attorney, at the clerk, and at the spectators. His calm is almost inhuman. Slowly, undisturbed and dispassionately at first, he begins to speak, saying,

"Yes. What I say is that I am innocent. That I am not only innocent, but in all my life I have never stole and I have never killed and I have never spilled blood. That is

184

what I want to say. And it is not all. Not only am I innocent of these two crimes, not only in all my life I have never stole, never killed, never spilled blood, but I have struggled all my life, since I began to reason, to eliminate crime from the earth.

"Now, I should say that I am not only innocent of all these things, not only have I never commited a real crime in my life—though some sins but not crimes—not only have I struggled all my life to eliminate crimes, the crimes that the official law and the official moral condemns, but also the crime that the official moral and the official law sanctions and sanctifies—the exploitation and the oppression of the man by the man, and if there is a reason why I am here as a guilty man, if there is a reason why you in a few minutes can doom me, it is this reason and none else."

Here, Vanzetti pauses—and seems to be groping in his memory for words and images. Then when he resumes his speech, the Judge is at a loss to understand what Vanzetti refers to. Only as Vanzetti goes on, does the aged, gaunt figure of Eugene Debs emerge from his words and enter the courtroom.

"I beg your pardon," Vanzetti says, gently now. "There is the most good man I ever cast my eyes upon since I lived, a man that will last and will grow always more near and more dear to the people, as far as into the heart of the people, so long as admiration for goodness and for sacrifice will last. I mean Eugene Debs.

"That man had a real experience of a court, of prison and of jury. Just because he want the world to be a little better he was persecuted and slandered from his boyhood to his old age, and indeed he was murdered by the prison. He

185

know our innocence, and not only he but every man of understanding in the world, not only in this country but also in the other countries, they all still stick with us, the flower of mankind of Europe, the better writers, the greatest thinkers of Europe, have pleaded in our favor. The scientists, the greatest scientists, the greatest statesmen of Europe, have pleaded in our favor. The people of foreign nations have pleaded in our favor.

"Is it possible that only a few on the jury, only two or three men, who would condemn their mother for worldly honor and for earthly fortune; is it possible that they are right against the world, the whole world has say it is wrong and that I know that it is wrong? If there is one that should know it, if it is right or if it is wrong, it is I and this man. You see it is seven years that we are in jail. What we have suffered during these seven years no human tongue can say, and yet you see me before you, not trembling, you see me looking you in your eyes straight, not blushing, not changing color, not ashamed or in fear.

"Eugene Debs say that not even a dog—something like that—not even a dog that kill the chickens would have been found guilty by American jury with the evidence that the Commonwealth have produced against us."

Now Vanzetti pauses—and stares into the Judge's eyes before he continues. This is the part of the dream that becomes a nightmare—even though at the time it happens, the Judge remains cold and collected as Vanzetti cries,

"We have proved that there could not have been another Judge on the face of the earth more prejudiced and more cruel than you have been against us. We have proved that. Still they refuse the new trial. We know, and you know in

186

your heart, that you have been against us from the very beginning, before you see us. Before you see us you already know that we were radicals, that we were underdogs.

"We know that you have spoke yourself and have spoke your hostility against us, and your despisement against us with friends of yours on the train, at the University Club of Boston, on the Golf Club of Worcester, Massachusetts. I am sure that if the people who know all what you say against us would have civil courage to take the stand, maybe your Honor—I am sorry to say this because you are an old man, and I have an old father—but maybe you would be beside us in good justice at this time.

"We were tried during a time that has now passed into history. I mean by that, a time when there was a hysteria of resentment and hate against the people of our principles, against the foreigner, and it seems to me—rather, I am positive of it, that both you and District Attorney have done all what it was in your power in order to agitate still more the passion of the juror, the prejudice of the juror, against us.

"The jury were hating us because we were against the war, and the jury don't know that it makes any difference between a man that is against the war because he believes that the war is unjust, because he hate no country, and a man that is against the war because he is in favor of the other country that fights against the country in which he is, and therefore a spy. We are not men of that kind. The District Attorney know that we were against the war because we did not believe in the purpose for which they say that the war was done. We believe it that the war is wrong, and we believe this more now after ten years be-

187

cause we understand it better day by day—the consequences and the result of the war. We believe more now than ever that the war was wrong, and I am glad to be on the doomed scaffold if I can say to mankind, 'Look out; you are in a catacomb of the flower of mankind. For what? All that they say to you, all that they have promised to you—it was a lie, it was an illusion, it was a cheat, it was a fraud, it was a crime. They promised you liberty. Where is liberty? They promised you prosperity. Where is prosperity? They have promised you elevation. Where is the elevation?'

"From the day I went in Charlestown Prison, the population of Charlestown Prison has doubled in number. Where is the moral good that the war has given to the world? Where is the spiritual progress that we have achieved from the war? Where are the security of life, the security of the things that we possess for our necessity? Where are the respect for human life? Where are the respect and the admiration for the good characteristics and the good of the human nature? Never as now before the war there have been so many crimes, so many corruptions, so many degenerations as there is now."

A pause now by the man in the court—the man in the Judge's dream, who speaks and pleads; and the Judge twists and turns and whimpers in his sleep. Yet he must listen again—and again.

"It was said," Vanzetti continues, his voice now the voice of a judge and not of a condemned felon, "that the defense has put every obstacle to the handling of this case in order to delay the case. I think it is injurious because it is not true. If we consider that the prosecution, the State, has employed one entire year to prosecute us, that is, one of the five years that the case has lasted was taken by the prosecution to begin our trial, our first trial. Then the defense make an appeal to you and you waited. I think that you had the resolve in your heart when the trial finished that you will refuse every appeal that we will put up to you. You waited a month or a month and a half and just lay down your decision on the eve of Christmas—just on the evening of Christmas. We do not believe in the fable of the evening of Christmas, neither in the historical way nor in the church way. You know some of our folks still believe in that, and because we do not believe in that, it don't mean that we are not human. We are human, and Christmas is sweet to the heart of every man. I think that you have done that, to hand down your decision on the evening of Christmas, to poison the heart of our family and of our beloved.

"Well, I have already say that I not only am not guilty of these two crimes, but I never commit a crime in my life— I have never steal and I have never kill and I have never spilt blood, and I have fought against the crime, and I have fought and I have sacrificed myself even to eliminate the crimes that the law and the church legitimate and sanctify."

Now, in the Judge's dream, Vanzetti's voice rises, fierce— awful, and searing the sleeping man like a hot iron.

"This is what I say: I would not wish to a dog or to a snake, to the most low and misfortunate creature of the earth—I would not wish to any of them what I have had to suffer for things that I am not guilty of. But my conviction is that I have suffered for things that I am guilty of. I am suffering because I am a radical and indeed I am a radical; I have suffered because I am an Italian, and indeed I am an Italian; I have suffered more for my belief than for myself; but I am so convinced to be right that if you could execute me two times, and if I could be reborn two other times, I would live again to do what I have done already.

"I have talk a great deal of myself but I even forget to name Sacco. Sacco too is a worker from his boyhood, a skilled worker, lover of work, with a good job and pay, a bank account, a good and lovely wife, two beautiful children and a neat little home at the verge of a wood, near a brook. Sacco is a heart, a faith, a character, a man; a lover of nature and of mankind. A man who gave all, who sacrifice all to the cause of liberty and to his love for mankind; money, rest, mundain ambitions, his own wife, his children, himself and his own life. Sacco has never dreamt to steal, never to assassinate. He and I have never brought a morsel of bread to our mouths from our childhood to today—which has not been gained by the sweat of our brows. Never.

"Oh, yes, I am a better babbler than he is, but many, many times in hearing his heartful voice ringing a faith sublime, in considering his supreme sacrifice, remembering his heroism, I felt small—small at the presence of his greatness and found myself compelled to fight back from my eyes the tears, and quench my heart trembling to my throat to not weep before him—this man called thief and assassin and doomed. But Sacco's name will live in the hearts of the people and in their gratitude when the District Attorney and your bones will be dispersed by time, when your name, his name, your laws, institutions, and your false god are but a *dim remembering of a cursed past in which man was wolf to the man. . . .*"

With those words, Vanzetti stops speaking. The impact of his last sentence is like a hammer smashed into the center of the silent courtroom. Now Vanzetti looks directly at the Judge, and his eyes are a huge and frightening part of the Judge's present nightmare.

"I have finished," Vanzetti says. "Thank you."

The Judge raps suddenly with his gavel, but there is no disorder, no sound for him to still. He lets go of the gavel and sees that his hand is trembling. He pulls himself together and says with forced firmness.

"Under the law of Massachusetts the jury says whether a defendant is guilty or innocent. The Court has absolutely nothing to do with that question. The law of Massachusetts provides that a Judge cannot deal in any way with the facts. As far as he can go under our law is to state the evidence.

"During the trial many exceptions were taken. These exceptions were taken to the Supreme Judicial Court. That Court, after examining all the exceptions—that Court in its final words said, 'The verdicts of the jury should stand; exceptions overruled.' That being true, there is only one thing that this Court can do. It is not a matter of discretion. It is a matter of statutory requirement, and that being true, there is only one duty that now devolves upon this Court, and this is to pronounce the sentences.

"First the Court pronounces sentence upon Nicola Sacco. It is considered and ordered by the Court that you, Nicola Sacco, suffer the punishment of death by the passage of a current of electricity through your body within the week beginning on Sunday, the tenth day of July, in the year of our Lord, one thousand, nine hundred and twenty-seven. This is the sentence of the law.

"It is considered and ordered by the Court that you, Bartolomeo Vanzetti—"

Vanzetti now leaps to his feet and cries out, "Wait a minute, please, your Honor. May I speak for a minute with my lawyer?"

"I think I should pronounce the sentence," the Judge continues. "Bartolomeo Vanzetti, suffer the punishment of death—"

Sacco interrupts him now with a sudden fierce cry, "You know I am innocent! That is the same words I pronounced seven years ago! You condemn two innocent men!"

But the Judge has gathered his nerve and his wits by now, and he goes on calmly,

"—by the passage of a current of electricity through your body within the week beginning Sunday, the tenth day of July, in the year of our Lord, one thousand, nine hundred and twenty-seven. This is the sentence of the law."

And then the Judge adds, "We will now take a recess."

And today, in the early evening of August 22nd, the day finally set for the execution after several delays, he woke up from his nap with those words of his echoing in his ears, *We will now take a recess.* He woke up and realized that someone was calling him for dinner. Actually, it was remarkable how little disturbed he was. He suddenly

192

had an appetite for food, and he realized with pleasure and relief that the day was already drawing to an end. When once it ended, this whole matter would be settled forever and soon forgotten. At least he consoled himself with this thought.

Chapter 14

THE LONGEST and most lonesome pilgrimages come to an end, and this day the Professor of Criminal Law had traveled across the universe and back. In the farthest reaches of space, he had gazed for brief moments at the deepest secrets of life, and what he found was bitter and unsettling. He had forgotten home and children, and when he ate, the food became coarse and tasteless in his mouth. He ate with the Attorney for the Defense, who had come into town for a last word or two with the men who were going to die. This attorney had stepped out of the case, in the hope that new legal aid might influence the Governor, but now he had come to Boston to speak once again with Bartolomeo Vanzetti. He had asked the Professor of Criminal Law to come with him to the death house in the State Prison.

"I am afraid," said the Professor of Criminal Law, saluting the dark companion at last. It had pursued him the whole day, and now stalked by his side. "I could not face Vanzetti."

"Why?" asked the Attorney. "It was not you who condemned him."

"No? But I'm not so sure of that any more. Do you remember the statement that Vanzetti made on the ninth of April, after the Judge passed sentence?"

The Attorney nodded, and the Professor added, with some embarrassment, "I would like to quote it to you. I have committed it to memory and have been carrying it around inside of me like a stone tied to my heart. I don't want to seem over-melodramatic, but this morning I faced the President of a great university—you know who I mean—and later, I saw a colored working man, beaten terribly because he walked on the picket line in front of the State House, and this and other things have been most unsettling. I need to see this thing clearly. I ask myself what Vanzetti meant when he said, 'If it had not been for these things, I might have live out my life talking at street corners to scorning men. I might have die, unmarked, unknown, a failure. Now we are not a failure. This is our career and our triumph. Never in our full life could we hope to do such work for tolerance, for justice, for man's understanding of man as now we do by accident. Our words—our lives—our pains—nothing! The taking of our lives—the lives of a good shoemaker and a poor fish peddler —all! That last moment belongs to us—that agony is our triumph.'

"What strange and brooding words those are, and how many times I have asked myself what they mean. I am not

195

sure that I know. Two men are going to die, and from now until the end, I will not lift my hand to prevent it."

"You cannot prevent it, my friend," the Attorney said. "You must understand that you and I can do nothing anymore."

"Is that the whole fruit that we suck on?" the Professor wondered. "The juice is sour, then. I am just a Jew and not even native to this land; but no one drags me into a police station and beats me until I am blind with blood. Yet all this black working man did was to walk on the picket line. I have done more. I bearded a great man of the old blood of this land, and practically called him a liar whose hands were dirty with blood—but no punishment came to me. Suddenly I see that the punishment is reserved for the oppressed, as Vanzetti calls them, and we smile about that, the quaintness of the term, but we are putting these two people to death because they are radicals, and not for any other reason. The mighty have been challenged, and for that challenge, a shoemaker and a fish peddler must pay with their lives. So why such a commotion, such a sound of voices? So many have died in silence, and you and I never raised a hand to do one damn thing about it. Now we try to heal our consciences, but a month from now we will live just as comfortably among the rich and the mighty. I will pay the small price of being fired out of the university, but in private practice I will make twice as much money—and my clients will be those who murdered Sacco and Vanzetti. Yet I try to say that my own hands are clean—"

The Attorney listening to him was a middle-aged man,

a Yankee of sober honesty and deep integrity, who had come into the case, not for money or fame, but because his irascible conscience led him into it; and now, for all that this kind of an outburst made him somewhat uneasy, he listened respectfully and thoughtfully. "I never accepted their views," he said. "I am a conservative man, and I never made a secret of that. But I don't whet my appetite with the smell of blood. They are being murdered, and it only fills me with shame that this should take place. But maybe, somehow, there is still hope. Come with me to the jail—do come."

With that and more argument, the Professor of Criminal Law finally agreed, and they walked in the summer evening past the State House, where the picket line still moved. As they came alongside of it, they were greeted by many of the people who marched, and the greeting was full of sadness. The tall young woman poet, whose name and verse were known all over the world, grasped the Defense Attorney's hand, begging him,

"You will do something? It's not too late, is it?"

"My dear, I will do what I can," he said.

Six women, walking together two by two, and weeping, carried signs which said, "We are textile workers from Fall River, Massachusetts. God help the mighty in New England if Sacco and Vanzetti die." On the sidewalk nearby, an old, gray-haired man held by hand a little boy, his grandchild, likely enough, and he whispered to the little boy, explaining and motioning; but when the child began to cry, the old man said worriedly, "No, no—it will not help for you to weep."

"We must not linger," the Attorney said, drawing the Professor along. "I have this appointment, and I must not be late."

"No, tonight is not a night to be late. You know, there never was anything like this before. Why? Why? I don't think that even when Jesus Christ carried his heavy cross to its destination, there was such grief from mankind. What will perish in us when these two go?"

"I don't know," said the Attorney somberly.

"Hope, perhaps?"

"I don't know. Shall I ask Vanzetti?"

"It would be too cruel."

"No, I don't think it would be cruel at all."

They took a cab to Charlestown. In a very plain tone of voice, the Attorney said to the Professor, "There, a block or two over on our right, is Winthrop Square—Austin Street, Lawrence Street, Rutherford Avenue, the persistence of names, so as to speak. Warren going into Henley—I've wondered if that is the same Warren, do you remember, 'Fear ye foes who kill for hire? Will ye to your homes retire—look behind you, they're on fire!' Am I quoting correctly? It must be thirty or forty years since I've seen that. And over that way, the monument—"

Only part of the Professor's attention was held by the words of the other. Both his thoughts and his emotions had responded to the serene quality of the early evening, the pastel beauty of the clouds in the sky acting as prisms for the light of the descending sun, the boats on the water, and all the many sounds and smells, the smell of the clean summer evening air, tinted and textured with smoke from the puffing locomotives, the sounds of train and boat whis-

198

tles and the mercilessly free passage of birds across the sky. All of it was so beautiful that it created a framework within which death was impossible and vile, and thus, for the moment, he lost all touch with the reality toward which they were moving. He was returned by the dry recollection of the Attorney, who spoke of monuments:

"You would have caught a glimpse of it a moment ago, but in the wrong place. Isn't that so? I've always been under the impression that the monument stands on Bunker Hill, but the battle was fought on Breed's Hill. That's where they dug their trenches and crawled into them, poor farmers and laborers facing the best regiments of Europe—"

"Men like Vanzetti?" the Professor asked.

"That doesn't disturb me, sir. No, really, no. The past is dead. I don't know what they were like—no one does now, I suppose. One thing I know, they were not people all alone like Sacco and Vanzetti—"

"Alone? Surely they are not alone—no." The Professor smiled slightly for the first time in hours. "They aren't alone."

"I know what you mean—I meant something else. You mean all the millions who weep for them. I've discovered that an ocean of tears will not move a small rock. A quarter of a million sign a petition, but what difference does it make?"

"I don't know," answered the Professor.

"There you have it. Up there on Bunker Hill, they had their guns in their hands. They underwrote their statement, sir."

"Don't you think they wept when Nathan Hale was hanged?"

"I feel like a schoolboy," the Attorney said to himself. "What old bones we are trying to rattle! Here is this Jew— they seem to recognize suffering, or maybe there's a bitter smell it leaves in the air—trying to find consolation somewhere. But the past is dead. He put his finger on it, and Sacco and Vanzetti are dying in a world they never made. We come as observers, but what else can we do?"

"There's the prison," the Professor said. The evening was golden, but he was filled with fears, and this portent of the beauty of the world, overlaid with a shimmering wash like a George Innes painting, only made the fears he carried with him sharper. There should have been thunder and lightning instead of this, but like a lady of infinite vanity, the world had arrayed herself in sheer perfection. They came up to the grim, octagonal walls of the prison, and for the first time, the Professor caught a glimpse of a further reality, and had insight into the profound meaning of John Donne's somber warning, "—never send to know for whom the bell tolls; it tolls for thee." He was going to his own death, for he was connected with the doomed men, his soul tied to theirs, his memory collective with theirs, his needs as theirs; and though in the years to come, he would forget this night and how he had died, for time does strange things, he would always have a touch of remembrance when he saw golden sunlight or felt the cold shadow of the angel of death passing by.

The Warden greeted them now with the professionally long countenance of a funeral parlor director, and within the prison the good light of day ended. They marched through crypt and catacomb toward the death house.

"I guess you understand that we don't welcome these

days," the Warden said. "These are bad days for a prison. Let me say that the whole population dies a little with the condemned, and that's not as fanciful as it might sound. There are little threads tying people together when they live in a jail."

"Howsoever you see the jail," thought the Professor.

"And how—how have they been?"

"Good," the Warden answered. "Within the situation, of course, but how good can anyone be at the end? They are two brave men, believe me, mister."

The Professor thought this came strangely from a warden, and peered at him uncertainly. The other lawyer had wrapped himself in his own defenses, and his slow steps paced with his memories of this case, a game at first, the way any complex legal case is a game, a puzzle, a problem and a challenge—and then finally, the focus of his life. Well, he had shaken loose from that. When all was said and done, people like Sacco and Vanzetti had always perished under one violence or another. They defied the great shibboleth and rose up to smash images. All other crimes might be forgiven, but the lord and master could not forgive him who cast doubt on lordliness and mastery. That was inevitable; therefore, why did the world protest so?

These thoughts were invaded by the advice of the Warden, who made it plain that to enter the death house on this day was not the least privilege extended by the Commonwealth of Massachusetts. Few people did it, and perhaps not for anyone else except these very two men.

"Do you know," the Professor of Criminal Law said wonderingly, "I have never seen either of them. I am going to see them for the first time now.

"You will find them two plain people," the Warden answered defensively.

"Yes—I'm sure. But you see, to me they have a legendary quality."

"I can understand that," said the Attorney for the Defense.

As they came to the wing which contained the death house, the Warden explained, "There are only three cells in the death house, and as you know, they are all three occupied. This is an unusual situation for us—but all three of these men are scheduled to die tonight. Unless, of course, there is a reprieve. Do you think there will be a reprieve?" he asked the Attorney for the Defense.

"I devoutly hope so."

"I tell them that they should hope, but I don't imagine there is too much hope," the Warden said. "When it has gone this far, it usually rolls on to the end. Now, as you see—I won't go in there with you; I don't go in there if I can help it—the three death cells are side by side, and then there is a passage into the room where the electric chair is. You wouldn't think that there would be protocol in such things, but if you have to do unpleasant things, you might as well do them systematically. If more than one man is going to die, they are placed in cells nearest to the chair in order of their scheduled death. It has been decided that if tonight we must go through with it, Madeiros will be executed first, then Sacco, and then Vanzetti. You will find them in the cells in that order. Please don't talk to anyone but Sacco or Vanzetti. The permission has been requested and granted for Sacco and Vanzetti, and I will have to hold you to that."

At first, the Professor of Criminal Law listened to this with cold horror, for it had not seemed possible that men should talk about these things in such a manner, so coldly and calmly, using the words they used in terms of the events they expected. It had seemed to him that such matters, this insane taking of human life, must be so vile that of necessity they were unspeakable and unmentionable, like unspeakable filth of the dirty underlife of some areas of mankind. At first, this was his reaction, but after a moment he realized that if such things take place, then there must needs be words to describe them; and that men who take part in such actions must use those words for want of others. The world was not monstrous secretly with a code language to describe its conditions; what was monstrous was openly monstrous, and the ordinary spoken language calmly fitted all such events. Nor did it stop with language; men, too, fitted into such events, even as he and his companion and colleague, both honorable men, had fitted into this ghastly world of granite walls and iron bars, walking calmly through it toward a house that had been constructed for only one reason—to take life legally. And for this purpose, this Christian and democratic civilization had devised a chair of metal and wood, into which a man could be strapped and held, while electric current of tremendous strength was directed through his body. Yet neither he nor his companion cried aloud with horror or grief; quite to the contrary—they behaved calmly and rationally, his friend saying,

"You may be quite at ease, Warden. I shall observe your rules scrupulously."

Then the Warden left them, and a prison guard took

them into the death house. They walked past the three cells, and as they passed each door, the Professor of Criminal Law looked in curiously—for a man must remain curious, even as he must breathe and sleep. First, he saw Madeiros, who stood in the center of his cell, motionless, thief and murderer waiting for death a few hours away. Then Sacco's cell. Sacco lay upon his bed, stretched out on his back, his eyes open and fixed on the ceiling. Then Vanzetti's cell, and Vanzetti waiting for them. He stood at the door of his cell, and he smiled and greeted them warmly and graciously—with a calm more terrible to the Professor than anything else that had happened in all that trying day.

The guard pointed to two wooden chairs which were set a little distance from the door of the cell. "Please sit there, gentlemen," he said. They sat down, but the Professor realized that by turning his head just a little, he could see the execution chamber and a corner of the chair itself. And no matter how hard he tried not to look that way, it drew his eyes.

It drew him away. The electric chair fixed him and held him to a point where he listened without hearing, and afterwards he could not, for his life, recall the details of the beginning conversation, except to remember that it concerned the release of all attorneys from the privilege of silence, so that no one of them might say that he reserved to himself any secret of the Sacco-Vanzetti case. All would be open and known to all men. This general thing, he recalled, but no more; he was held and obsessed by a prying wonder about the instrument of death, and the whys and wherefores of it and others like it. When it was so simple to open a vein or drink a cup of poison, as Socrates had, why must man's ingenuity endlessly devise machines, a guillotine, an automatic gallows, a gas chamber, an electric chair?

"In all my life, as I remember, my friend, I do not think I do a crime which a man is ashamed of, or even a small action which is dastardly," Vanzetti was saying. "It is not that I am a more good man than others, but a plain man, and this is true about plain men. So you need not worry about my innocence. I am innocent."

Now the words of the Attorney came back to the Professor. He had put it more or less in this fashion—that though he was fully convinced of the innocence of Sacco and Vanzetti, he desired now, in this last hour, a statement to that effect, so that he might utterly refute those who destroyed two innocent men.

"Oh, the horror, the damned, callous ego of such a question!" the Professor thought; nevertheless, Vanzetti had answered it as gently and kindly as if this philosophical conversation were taking place before the warm hearth of a man with many good decades before him.

It was with curious if sorrowful eyes that the Professor observed Bartolomeo Vanzetti, the high, balding forehead, majestic and commanding, the fine brows, the deep-set eyes, the long, straight nose, the full, drooping mustache, and just visible beneath it, the wide and sensitive mouth and the gently-shaped chin. "What a handsome man!" the Professor thought. "What a splendor in his poise and features! He stands there like a king, but the pride is utterly without aloofness. What makes such a man? Where does he come from, standing with such damned dignity and waiting for death?"

And as if in answer to his thoughts, Vanzetti addressed him, saying how glad he was to meet him, and thanking him for what he had done on the case.

"What I did was nothing."

"Nothing—no, much. When I think how men like you come and join with Sacco and me, my heart overflows. Believe me.

"Believe me," he repeated, now speaking to the Attorney, "I wish I can say what gratitude I have for all you do for me. I cannot express it fully. You want me to hope now, but I know better. Sacco knows better. Tonight we will die. I am afraid to die, but I am also prepare to die. Not once, but a thousand time, Sacco and myself already die— we are prepare. This is for the cause of mankind, to make an end of man's oppression of other men. I am filled with sadness, for I never again see sister or family or anyone I love; but not sadness alone. There is also triumph, for men will remember what we suffer—and fight better for a just world."

"I wish I could believe what you believe, Bartolomeo," the Attorney said.

"Why should you? How could you? You see here Van·zetti who awaits death. The man is finish—but what went into making the man before he is finish? I call myself now a class conscious man, but I was not born that way. I am born like you, and then when I grow to man, I know little enough. All my years in America, I work like three men, and always I have nothing. But in my heart become a great love for the people who labor beside me. I stop being just Italian. I think, these are my people. Then I work in brickyard in Connecticut and then at stone pit

206

in Meriden. Two years, I work pick and shovel and crow-bar in stone pit, and there I learn beautiful dialect of Tuscany because Tuscans work there—but the boss hate, no matter what speech we talk, just work, you damn wops. American man work next to me, and he say to me one day, Hey, Barto, there are two languages, one for boss, one for you and me, and he smile at me and my whole heart go out to him. So I learn that class consciousness not a phrase invented by propagandists, but a real vital force. It comes inside of me, and I stop being animal, a work beast, and I become human being. Then this American talk, always saying, Look at your hands, Barto. All the world is make with your hands, but always someone else take. Even the gun *you* make to kill your brother with, but he who take the bread you bake, *he* make nothing, nothing, Barto, nothing. Just look at your hands, Barto—he say. Oh, what a strength in them hands. But not all at once do I understand, but little by little. Now they kill me because I understand that men will some day live like brothers—well, I am not only one must die for that understanding. But you are out there, my friend. Why should you believe what I believe? I am a worker—always."

"I am not against you," the Attorney said. "Bartolomeo, you must understand that I am not against you. But I don't see any solution to all this with bitterness and hatred."

"You don't want me to be bitter," Vanzetti said. "Should my heart be filled with love for enemy who bring me to moment of my death?"

"After this, there could be violence and hatred, and death piled upon death. Do you want that, Bartolomeo?"

"Did I ever want that?" Vanzetti now asked, with just

a slight smile. "We were brought into the courtroom, and there Judge speak that we are people of violence. The District Attorney—he tell the jury, these are terrible, bad and violent men. But where is one little bit of violence that Sacco and me ever lift his hand to? Have we ever hurt man? Is it violence to go to our brothers who are workers and say to them, Maybe for him you bake the whole bread, it is not fair you should eat only the crust? No—look, the violence is done to me. For seven year locked up in prison, tortured, treated like criminal—seven long year in dungeon. That is violence. No such terrible violence was ever done to any human being than you do to gentle Sacco and to me. We are selected and told we have committed terrible crimes in a place where we never go and never even see with our eyes. Then we are tried and cursed and slandered, and for years and years locked away in prison cell. This is violence. For every other human being, one death is enough—but for Sacco and me, a thousand death, and still it is not enough. But day after day we must die again and again. You I respect as good man and friend, but how can you come here and beg me against violence? I never make violence. Is there ever a time in the whole world when some man stand up for brotherhood and a better life, when he is not accused of violence? So with Jesus Christ. I do not compare Sacco and myself with Jesus Christ, and I am also not religious man. But you people who take Christ's name and call yourself Christian, you never stop crucifying."

Now the Attorney demanded, his voice low and shaken for the first time, "Bartolomeo, do you turn against me? Have I done these things? Did I spare myself in my effort to win your freedom and to prove an innocence that I knew?"

"No, I don't turn against you. Never do I turn against friend or comrade—this you know. But why does this terrible slander of violence follow us here to death house? Do you think I want to die? I tell you this—a reporter was here from a labor newspaper, a good man who I trust with all my heart, and I plead and beg him, he should come back with a revolver for me so that they will not take me out of here like sheep, but I can fight and go down fighting in human dignity, instead of being led to slaughter like cattle. But he could not come back, or maybe won't come back of his own will—and that is the only violence I ever think of. But it is always the cry of violence from the clean and noble good citizen who say, They must die because they make violence against me. Christ must die because he make violence. Galileo must die because he make violence. Giordano Bruno—yes, and Lenin too, they say he is a man to make violence and push away what is legal and right. I ask you now, what is legal and right—to kill Sacco and Vanzetti, is that legal and right?"

"Have I ever said that, Bartolomeo? The last word has not been said concerning right and wrong. I believe in an Almighty God who balances such matters on His own scales, and never will I accept the decision that there is no appeal beyond the Governor of Massachusetts."

Now Vanzetti's voice dropped and became muted and full of loneliness. "Do you believe that?" he asked. "It is not my belief. I sometimes ask myself, how is it so many good men do not believe in your God, in your judgment day? And them who believe—they fear death just as much."

"Nevertheless," said the Attorney, "I believe firmly and unshakably that there is a life after this one."

The Professor of Criminal Law looked at his companion. There was no doubt in the Attorney's voice, there was no doubt in the way he now looked at Vanzetti. He was an upright man, the Attorney, and stiffened all over with pride and unshakability. He had fought all through the last phases of this case, yet it had not shaken him. His firm faith and belief was in himself, his friends, his caste and his class, his personal philosophy and fortune and money in the bank—and in all of that, he was not shaken, and now he stated his belief in life eternal. In a certain way, the Professor of Criminal Law envied this Attorney; for the Professor of Criminal Law had no faith that was unshaken tonight, nor could he at this moment stiffen himself with pride or security. Yet when he raised his eyes from the Attorney to Bartolomeo Vanzetti, he saw that the one was not less sure than the other. Even in his last words, Vanzetti's voice had not quivered or broken. He still maintained his calm, and the large sculptured planes and angles of his noble head still reflected an almost indescribable serenity. It was this serenity which all through this interview had plucked at the Professor's memory, stirred it, and dug into it to awaken something of long, long ago. Again and again, a response to this astonishing serenity approached the Professor's threshold of consciousness, and the words were almost upon his lips; and then, again and again, the memory receded and became unobtainable.

The Professor of Criminal Law sorely desired to be able to say something here and now that might offer a little different substance to Vanzetti than what he had already received. The Professor was not at all certain that this was not the last contact of the two doomed men with the outside world, and he felt a great sense of frustration that this contact should be limited to the conversation that had already taken place. He knew enough of the everyday commonness of life and living to understand that no mighty sayings would emerge in the few minutes that were left to them; and yet he kept thinking—also as a part of that poorly pursued recollection which provokingly touched at the edge of his consciousness—that some particular and splendid phrases might arise, bearing within them the life substance of these two men, assuring them of the only immortality in which he himself was certain he believed.

Vanzetti still groped with thoughts of violence. "I find it strange," he was saying, "that you should come here and warn me against violence. I stand here in a cell, waiting for death to come to me, but you approach and plead for no violence. Have I magical powers to order up violence out of nothing? Such powers I do not have. Violence comes when too much weight is loaded onto back of people. What kind of world have you made? Is it world without violence? At the trial, District Attorney curse Sacco and me because we will not fight in war where twenty million human souls are slain. Yet Sacco and Vanzetti are charged with violence. What a world you make where so few live with the sweat and suffering of so many! Your whole world is violence. You are my friend, and believe me, I love you and honor what you do for me, but also I know it is your world and not the world of Sacco and me. Some day it will be different, but without violence? I do not know. You crucify Christ not once, but again and again, whenever he

211

come to you. Sacco listen to every word I say, and Sacco is plain man who talk English poorly, but Sacco is like Jesus Christ himself for pureness and goodness, and in a little while, Sacco must die—"

The Professor of Criminal Law was not able to listen to any more of this, endure any more, or hear any more of this. The mechanism in his ears still functioned, but by a dogged psychological process he was able to remove himself from the meaning of the sound. Now only the memory which he sought concerned him, until finally, like a person in a trance, he came to himself and to the realization that the interview was finished. He shook hands with Vanzetti and was somewhat surprised to discover that the flesh was warm and that the clasp was firm—and close by, he looked into the brown eyes of the man.

"Good-by, and thank you, my friend," Vanzetti said, but the Professor was not able to speak now—not until they were outside of the prison walls, when the Attorney reminded him with some surprise that he had remained silent all through the trying incident. But now the Professor had found what he had been seeking in his memory, and he was able to say, "When we heard this, we were ashamed, and restrained our tears."

"I am afraid I don't understand you," the Attorney said, himself overwrought and deeply disturbed by what they had been through.

"No? I'm sorry," the Professor said. "I had been trying to remember something, and now I remember it."

"It sounded familiar," the Attorney said mechanically.

"Yes—do you recall, 'Thus far, most of us were with difficulty able to restrain ourselves from weeping, but when we saw him drinking, and having finished the draught, we could do so no longer; but in spite of myself the tears came in full torrent, so that, covering my face, I wept for myself, for I did not weep for him, but for my own fortune, in being deprived of such a friend'?"

The Attorney nodded heavily. Now the two men stood waiting in the twilight for the car which the Warden had promised he would send round to take them across the river into the city. The words of the Professor of Criminal Law had pricked at the Attorney's own memory, whereupon he wondered aloud, "What was it Socrates said then? Do you remember?"

" 'I have heard that it is right to die with good omens. Be quiet therefore and bear up.' "

And seeing that now tears ran down the Professor's cheeks, and seeing how he stood there in the lowering evening, hunched over like a great, ugly, hurt animal, the Attorney for the Defense forbore to ask any more questions or to make any additional conversation.

Chapter 15

Now Vanzetti stood at the door of his cell, held there by his own thoughts and by the silent echo of all that he had just finished saying; but the two other men lay each of them upon his cot, each of them upon his back, each of them with wide, vacant eyes probing into the frightful mystery of the close, close future.

Vanzetti held his hands in front of him, fingers curled around the bars in the opening of his cell door. He looked upon his hands which were himself, and he raised again in his mind the eternal question of how it would be when his whole person, his being and his knowingness became nothing, without memory or awakening. Fear blew over him like a cold and irresistible wind from which he tried vainly to shelter himself; now he no longer wanted a delay or postponement in the execution; his despair being such that if a thought could have brought about his own death, he would have wished the end and finished living. But thinking of himself that way made him think of Sacco, and he knew that what he suffered, Sacco also suffered. His heart went out in great pity to Sacco, and he called to him.

"Nicola, Nicola, do you hear me?"

Wide-eyed, Sacco dreamed in his wakefulness, his thoughts voyaging back like a boat driving through a sea of sorrow. Everything turned into its opposite; if he recalled gladness filled with laughter, within him it turned into unhappiness wet with tears. He would yearn to remember a particular thing, but the moment this sought-for vision recreated itself within his mind, he sought to drive it away. He remembered all the times when, with his wife, Rosa, he had taken part in this or that amateur dramatic performance. Rosa was beautiful and gracious and talented; and he had always felt that she should have been a famous actress. He had always known how wonderful she was, and never had he understood the mystery which surrounded the action she took in marrying him. He had always firmly believed that no one else understood it either, and that one and all said, "Just think and try to understand how that beautiful Rosa has married Nick Sacco. Now what does she see in him?" To which, no doubt, someone else answered, "Have you ever known it to fail—plain women marry the handsome men, and men of the most exceeding plainness, the most beautiful women. It has to be that way, and life levels out that way. If not for that fortunate provision of nature, you would have two races coming into being—the very beautiful and the very plain."

In any case, she had married him, and each night he repeated the substance of the miracle to himself in terms of both realization and gratitude.

"It is my Rosa who has married me," he would say to

himself, "plainly and evidently."

Now he repeated it to himself, and it stabbed into him like physical pain squeezing his already-tortured heart. When he drove this pain away, a new scene replaced it. He and Rosa had given a concert in a simple arrangement of *The Divine Comedy*. They had worked it out themselves in the most obvious manner, and yet it was effective. For example, when Rosa would say,

> "Nor when poor Icarus felt the hot wax run,
> Unfeathering him, and heard his father calling,
> 'Alack! alack! thou fliest too high, my son!'"

Sacco would answer:

> "Than I felt, finding myself in the void falling
> With nothing but air all around, nothing to show,
> No light, no sight but the sight of the beast appalling."

Again he flung this agonizing thought from him, wondering why his mind had sought and selected the honey-liquid Italian of just those two verses. It became more than he could bear, and he turned over onto his stomach, burying his face in the tear-dampened palms of his hands, and crying into his hands, "Rosa, Rosa, Rosa—" until he had fought through the spasm of grief and fear, and once again memory returned, offering him this time the recollection of strikes and picket lines and places where working people met to consider what a handful of poor people could do, with no union and no unity. He tried to separate all these things in his memory in order to file each one, but there were so many strikes and so many picket lines, so many occasions—the machine workers at Hopedale, the shoe workers at Milford, the textile workers at Lawrence, the pale men and women from the paper mills. He saw again the aftermath of each tiny meeting where the hat was passed around and a collection was taken. It was then his habit and practice to crumple a five dollar bill in his palm so that no one could see it or know how much it was and thereby feel ashamed or mortified because they had to give less—and having done this, to drop the bill into the hat.

Those were days when he was earning from sixteen to twenty-two dollars a day, working overtime as a finely skilled shoe worker. It was more than enough money for all their needs, and Rosa too would say, "Yes, yes, help them, help them. These are your good comrades." But for all that the job brought in twenty-two dollars a day, he resigned and threw it away when the war began, and talked it through with Rosa for all of one night, his feeling that he would die, lay down his life, kill himself before he would take up a gun and shoot down a fellow worker, German or Hungarian or Austrian or anything else.

Rosa had understood. A quality which had entered into their relationship from the very beginning was the immediate and deep understanding on the part of each of them of the problems of the other. Many people, friends of his, said, "Oh, Sacco—Sacco is a simple and easy-going man." Perhaps he was; but this made him feel more deeply, not less deeply, and in that way his wife was just as simple and direct. They merged together. Whenever Sacco saw men and women who were not getting along together, scrapping and biting at each other all the time, he was filled with a

217

terrible sense of pity, just as when he saw someone crippled badly. He knew men who committed adultery, but to his way of thinking, they were driven like mad animals.

He had only to look at Rosa. Not that their marriage always went like a dream of romantic love. They would grow angry at each other, fight with each other, be silent toward each other—but always it broke and everything poured out and nothing was concealed. It was a condition of equality as well as frankness, for neither ever excluded the other, and to their friends they always seemed like two children, in love and bound as comrades at one and the same time.

This condition seemed to Vanzetti the most wonderful thing between two human beings that he had ever seen—particularly the grave and straightforward manner in which Sacco dealt with his wife. One day Vanzetti had come to their home and, finding the house empty—they never locked their door, feeling that if anyone needed their few poor possessions, he was more than welcome to them—he sat down in the shade of the front to wait for them to return. Vanzetti sat in the corner made by steps and wall, sunk in the shadow, comfortable and cool on that summer afternoon, and unobserved by Sacco and Rosa as they returned.

It happened that at that time, Rosa was growing heavy with the first child, and for that reason they walked very slowly; but, as is the case with so many women, the pregnancy had cast a glow all over her, a tint upon her beauty as if there were light spread thinly everywhere under her skin. She and Sacco held hands, and as they walked, they turned their heads every so often to smile at each other. It was a gesture so simple and natural that Vanzetti was quite overcome by it; and, as he said afterwards, he was filled with the desire to weep for the plain joy of such happiness.

Sacco had his own memory of that day. They had walked down to Stilton Brook and had taken off their shoes and stockings and sat on a rock with their feet in the water. They sang together the delightful song which had been written for so foolish a purpose as to celebrate the opening of a cable railroad in Italy, and then they talked about a name for their child.

"If it is a boy," he said, taking up the favorite and endless discussion, "Antonio."

'No." They had agreed on Dante already. "Why do you always change?"

"Maybe it will be twins, and then we will need two names."

"No. It will not be twins."

"A girl?"

"I thought you agreed that Ines is the most beautiful name in the world."

"Rosa is."

"Nick," she had said then, "just suppose someone was listening to us saying the most foolish things anyone could dream of saying, like two little children who have just fallen in love. We have too much. Bite your fist."

He bit his hand, and Rosa began to cry.

"Why—why are you crying?"

"I filled up inside," she said simply.

He kissed her, and she stopped crying. They sat for a while. They walked back through a field of wild flowers, and he picked buttercups and snapdragons and Indian paintbrush and daisies, like a little boy, twisting all the flowers into a wreath for her hair. Then, hand in hand, they came walking back to their house, where finally they spied Vanzetti sitting in the shade; and suddenly he, Sacco, was overwhelmed with a sense of his own riches and Vanzetti's aloneness, and he thought,

"Poor Barto—poor, poor Barto."

Once again the piercing agony of pain bit through recollection. Sacco sank his teeth into the edge of his palm, biting harder and harder, in the hope that one pain might shut out another. And it was through this cloud of misery that Vanzetti's voice came to him, the calm and even and reassuring tones of Vanzetti calling to him,

"Nicola, Nicola, do you hear me? Nicola, are you there, and what are you doing? Tell me, dear friend."

Sacco sat up on his cot, driving away memories and the past as one drives off one's enemy—and he tried to answer his friend in the same voice his friend had used, but for him it was not possible to speak without grief. All he could say was,

"Here I am, Barto."

And then he added, a moment later, in sudden panic, "Barto, Barto, what time do you think it is? What time has it become already?"

"Some time between eight and nine o'clock," Vanzetti answered, speaking in Italian. "Not early enough to torture us too much with the waiting, but then again, neither is it late enough for us to give up hoping."

"What do you hope for?" Sacco asked. "I have used up all my power to hope, Barto. This time I know it is the

220

end and the finish, and I don't care any more. I don't want to hope. I only want it to be over."

"Nicola, such a way to talk!" said Vanzetti, almost lightly. "Are our chances any worse than those of someone with a terrible illness? To tell you the truth, I think our chances are better. Our difficulty is to imagine what is happening outside. We begin to think that we are alone. Loneliness is our enemy. Instead of that, try to think of how it must be everywhere, how many hundreds of thousands of working people have our names upon their lips and will not allow us to die. I put my life in their hands, Nicola. That is why I am so calm. You can hear in my voice, can't you, how calm I am? That is the reason why. Millions stand around us and support us."

"I can hear the calm in your voice," Sacco agreed, "but I cannot understand it."

"It is a very simple thing to understand," Vanzetti said. "I have developed good eyes of my own, and they can see over the few pieces of stonework that this prison consists of. You know, Nicola, there will some day be a race of people on this earth who will look back upon this miserable, dirty jail as you and I look back on a straw hut that savages live in. I have eyes to see that plainly, and the knowledge with which to understand it. I tell you that, Nick—and I am not saying this just to pick up my courage and yours—I am better off now than when first I came to this country. Then my eyes were younger, and there were no prison walls around me, but I saw nothing. First I went to work as a dish washer in an exclusive men's club in New York, where the rich came to spend the hours they had no other way of filling. Sixteen hours a day I worked

221

in the heat and in the darkness, washing dishes, breathing in the filth and the steam and the lousy smells, and even when I raised up my eyes, they saw nothing. From that job to other jobs—dish washer, day laborer, pick and shovel and crowbar to turn the rocks over with—selling my body and my youth and my strength for two dollars a day, three dollars a day—yes, and once, Nick, once, believe me, for sixty cents a day and a rotten plate of stew! When I looked around me then, I saw nothing but hopelessness. There were walls everywhere, thicker and higher than the walls around this prison. But now, so help me, my eyes can see into the future. I, Bartolomeo Vanzetti—I could not live forever, no matter. Sooner or later I would die. But this way, I tell you, you and I, Nick, we live forever and our names will never be forgotten."

In his cell, the thief listened, not understanding all of it, but picking up a thread here and there through the poor Portuguese and little Italian that he was able to speak and understand. And he cried out like a child,

"And where will I be, Bartolomeo? Where will I be in that future?"

"Poor man," Vanzetti said. "Poor man."

Madeiros came to the door of his cell, and now he pleaded in turn, "What is for me, Barto? In all my life I never before knew two people like you. You two are the first in my whole life who talk kindly to me, and decently, as if I were a human being and not an animal. But what sense does it make, Barto? From the very beginning I never had a chance."

"That is right. From the very beginning you never had a chance."

"I listen to Sacco. Sacco tells me how he had a garden, how he was up every morning at four to dig in his garden, and how each night after he had come back from the plant, he dug in the garden again until the sun set. I listen to Sacco and he makes a picture for me of a man with his arms full of newly harvested fruit which he gives to those who need it and who have no fruit of their own. But all I harvested, Barto, was the dry grass and the withered weeds."

"A crop you never sowed," Sacco said now. "Poor thief—a crop you never planted."

"Then are you two my friends?" Madeiros asked.

"What a thing to ask!" Vanzetti replied. "Can't you see how it is here, Celestino? We are three of us bound together with everlasting ties. In a few hours we will walk out of here, and the whole world will say, Sacco and Vanzetti and a thief have perished. But here and there across the world, in their own hearts, men will know that three human beings were slain. We crawl one little step closer to an understanding of it."

"But," protested Madeiros, "I am guilty and you are innocent. If there is one man in the whole world who knows that you are innocent, it is I—I tell you, it is I, and I know it!"

Now he was carried away by his own emotion and passion, and now he beat with his fists against the door of his cell, screaming at the top of his lungs, "Innocent, innocent—do you hear me! Innocent! Here are two men who are innocent! I know! I am Madeiros, thief and murderer! I sat in the car that drove into South Braintree! I was a part of the crime and a part of the murder! I know

223

the faces and the names of those who killed! You are murdering innocent men!"

"Easy, easy," said Vanzetti. "Easy, poor lad. What good is it? Talk in a softer voice, and the whole world will hear you, I swear to you."

"And gently, my son," Sacco said. "Gently and softly like Barto tells you. Listen to Barto. He is a very wise man, the wisest man I ever knew in my whole life. He is right when he says that if you talk softly the whole world will hear you."

Madeiros stopped screaming, but he still remained pressed to the door of his cell. His bitter weeping, his grief, his frustration and hopeless sorrow had a profound effect upon the two men who were in the cells alongside of his. Each of them felt like a father to this poor, hapless thief. Each of them was thinking in the same terms—of a lad who was born blind into the world and never opened his eyes. Their own paths were man-made, and as they looked back upon their lives, each of them could identify, step by step, the willful and thoughtful actions which had brought him finally to this conclusion. Yet they understood that Madeiros could not do this, that for Madeiros it was predestined and inevitable, a bitter, shrunken seed planted in soil someone else had plowed.

In response to Madeiros' screams, two guards came running, and with them, a prison hospital attendant; but Vanzetti told them that it would be all right, and that they should go away.

"Screaming like that—" one of the guards began to say.

"You too would scream," Vanzetti interrupted him

harshly, "if you could count the minutes and the seconds before you must die. Now leave us alone."

Now both he and Sacco began to talk to Madeiros. For the next half-hour they talked to him, gently and wisely and with great concern. In a sense, Madeiros had given them a most precious gift indeed; for in their concern for him, they forgot for a moment their own awful fear. Sacco spoke to Madeiros of his home, of his wife and of his two children. He told little amusing anecdotes about very small things, as, for instance, the first time his son, Dante, had smiled, and how it feels to see a smile on the face of an infant only six or seven weeks old.

"It is like the soul breaking through," he said to Madeiros. "It is there all the time, but suddenly, like a flower well-watered in a world of sunshine, its petals open."

"You believe that men have souls?" Madeiros whispered.

Vanzetti answered him. Vanzetti was filled with wisdom and tenderness, and during the past few days he had lived for many hundreds of years. Whereupon, he pointed out to Madeiros how long men have been trying to answer this question.

"Is man a beast?" he asked softly. "My son, we must see this—that very often, those who talk most of God, treat their own fellow men as if God was an impossibility. The way they treat man, he has no soul, for their very treatment of him is proof of that. But just think of how the three of us here are bound together, and in what kind of a compact. Here we are, yourself, Madeiros, who grew up in all the bitter misery of the streets and the alleys of Providence. You were a thief and you killed men. And here alongside of you is Sacco, who is the best man I have ever known, a good shoemaker, a good worker. And I, Vanzetti, who tried to be a leader for my fellow workers. You would think that we are three very different people, but when you come down to it, depend upon it, we are as alike as three peas in a pod. We have a soul which joins us together and then joins itself with millions—and when we die, there will be a stab in the heart of all mankind, and such a spasm of pain that I weep to think of it. In that way, no one ever dies. Do you understand me, Celestino?"

"I cannot tell you how I am trying," the thief answered. "In all my life I never tried so hard to understand anything."

Now Sacco said, "Celestino, Celestino—I never asked you this before, but tell me now. When you made your confession of the crime at South Braintree, was it because you knew that you would die anyway for the other crimes you made, and therefore had nothing to lose, or was it because of us?"

"I can tell you the truth about that," Madeiros answered. "First I read about you and Vanzetti in the newspapers, and you can't imagine how long I thought of it and tried to understand why they were so eager to kill you. Then one day your wife came to visit you, and I caught just a glimpse of her. Then I said to myself, I will do something so that Sacco doesn't die, and as for myself, I care nothing about what happens to me. That's the truth of it. Maybe in the whole world there is no one who would believe me, maybe not even my own mother if she was alive. Now I am telling the truth. If there is one time in a man's whole life that he tells the truth simply and plainly, it is at a time like this. So I tell you that I felt that maybe with a new trial, I would not be found guilty of murder. But I knew that once I made this confession to what happened at South Braintree, then it was all lost and I would have to die. I knew that, but still I had to make the confession, I had to tell what really happened."

"Ah!" cried Vanzetti. "There you have something. See, my friend Nicola, see how that is. What is there more that a human being can do than to lay down his life for another? That is why we are perishing. We give our lives as hostages for the working class, but what of Madeiros? Look at poor Madeiros, and think how it is with him. He gave his life for us, just as simply as that. Celestino, tell me, why did you do it? Can you tell me that?"

"Do you know," the thief said simply, "I have asked myself the same question a hundred times. I don't know how to speak the answer, but sometimes I feel the answer plainly."

Chapter 16

AT NINE O'CLOCK the Priest came. By birth, all three of the men in the death house were Roman Catholics, but Sacco and Vanzetti had already made it plain that they neither desired nor were in need of this kind of help. Whereupon, the Priest came for Celestino Madeiros, thief and murderer, and the Warden brought him into the lonely, death-stilled chamber.

As the clock ticked away the final minutes and hours of August 22nd, and as the moment of execution approached, people who were connected with it in any way whatsoever reflected this change, this irrevocable shrinking of time. If it caused a grim stiffening in the strange conviction of the Governor of Massachusetts, then on the other hand it also caused a softening in the reserve of a Chinese mother whose husband was a sweeper in the streets of Peking—and her tears reflected the bitter shrinkage of time. If the President of the United States went to sleep quite easily, with nothing that one could count or calculate upon his conscience, then a copper miner in Chile ate his crust of bread somberly, tasted nothing of its nourishment, and knew only that his heart grew heavier and heavier. And in the Massachusetts State Prison too, the souls of men withered a little more each hour, and their faces became grayer.

"I will walk in there with you," said the Warden to the Priest. "But I tell you, Father, what I would not say to anyone else for all the world, that this little walk becomes my punishment, and I have no gratitude for the fate that made me warden of a prison."

The Priest slowed his steps to the steps of the man who guided him. The Priest knew the various ways of death, the measured pace, the unique cadence, the strange, slow dance to mournful music. He had come close to death in many a place and on many an occasion, but out of this increasing knowledge came no increasing intimacy. The hooded one was not his friend, nor had his own fear been conquered at any point along the way. What he had learned in familiarity was balanced by the truer estimate he was able to make of this dark adversary; and as he now walked through the familiar and dreary corridors of the State Prison, he went over in his own mind the possibilities which presented themselves to him on this unenviable mission of conversion.

It had been put to him that there was joy in far off places for the triumph of a soul saved; but marching here in these tunnels of stone, he could not quite visualize the joy in radiant halls if he should succeed in the conversion of Sacco and Vanzetti or of a poor, damned thief. He rehearsed in his mind fragments of conversation which he speculated upon having now with Sacco and Vanzetti. But each time, the Priest retreated from this possibility which he himself had erected; and out of his debate with himself, he came to a decision not to venture where angels feared to tread and attempt to scale the heights separating him from the two lonely radicals, but rather to concentrate his fire where there would be less resistance—in the direction of the soul of the thief and murderer, Celestino Madeiros.

Guilts would not plague him for this choice, for was it not plainly evident that the sin of Sacco and Vanzetti was perhaps venal beyond forgiveness or reclamation? These two men were the point of the long tongue of the red dragon, the peculiar monster of this priest's time, the beast —as he now saw it—which lapped with a gaping and fanged maw at all the sweetness and succulence of Europe.

Equal and more rejoicing would arise at the thought that a thief and murderer—crimes not so bad, certainly, as those others—had confessed himself and sought absolution.

Yet the Priest would have had to be insensitive indeed not to be reminded, as he walked with the Warden toward the death house, of the singular parallel presented here; for here were two men whom millions loved, and who were to be crucified, and between them there was a thief who would also die; and blasphemous thought though he might conceive it to be, the Priest could not forbear comparing this finality with the finality of Jesus Christ—who also died because the State desired it, and who also was not alone in his agony, but was accompanied into whatever future there was by two thieves. And thinking this, the Priest said to himself,

"Well, who knows but that this man, Celestino Madeiros, has been placed here for a purpose, and who knows but that I too am sent to him for a purpose?—and while I do not know the whole of this purpose, I can unquestionably see glimmerings of a pattern. Being neither a Bishop nor a Cardinal, I will follow the pattern where it leads me, without trying to understand it too well." And he turned to the Warden and said,

"It will do no good to approach Sacco and Vanzetti again?"

"It will do no good, and I do not think we have any right to."

"Then my mission is for the thief," the Priest nodded, and he walked the rest of the way in silence until he came to the three cells of Death Row. Here the air was so permeated with inevitability and so chilled with misery, that the Priest stayed close to the Warden, hugging his human presence for reassurance, and following him to the door of Madeiros' cell, where the Warden said,

"Celestino, I have brought you a priest so that you may talk with him and prepare yourself for the end, if, indeed, the end must come."

Past the Warden, the Priest could see into the simple orderliness of Madeiros' cell. There was a cot, and a few books, and nothing else. Here in this place, man left the world as propertyless and as naked as he entered into it. Also, out of the corner of his eye, the Priest had glimpses of the cells of Sacco and Vanzetti, but he resolutely turned his eyes away, steeling himself for this one task which would now require all of his strength.

Madeiros sat upon his bed. He sat rather calmly, with his head up, nor did he turn to look at the door of his cell when the Warden's voice came to him. Watching him, the

Priest wondered whether he knew that it was already past nine o'clock, and that already, time and hope for this world had abandoned him. If, indeed, Madeiros knew this, he gave no sign of undue disturbance, and he said, quite calmly,

"I wish to thank you, and also the Priest, but send him away. I don't want him and I don't need him."

"Has he been like this all day?" whispered the Priest to the Warden. "So calm and so unperturbed?"

"By no means," the Warden whispered back, puzzled himself as to how to account for the present demeanor of Madeiros. "This is very new. From early this morning, he has been upset and sometimes hysterical, and sometimes screaming with fear and horror at the top of his lungs, the way a pig screams when the first blow of the hammer tells it that death is in process."

"Well, what now?" asked the Priest.

"You can talk to him if you wish," the Warden replied.

How does one grapple for the soul of a murderer?" the Priest asked himself, for this particular chore had never been his before. "Where does one enter combat?" And then he decided that he would ask the question of Madeiros as simply and as directly as Madeiros had answered him, saying to the lad,

"And why don't you want a priest, my son?"

Now Madeiros raised his head, turned his eyes toward the cell door, and faced the Priest with a glance so clear and fixed in its intentness that it drove against him like a level lance, tumbling him down from his precious towers of righteousness and doctrine—to a level where he saw before him only a boy who was now waiting for his death without

232

fear. The wonder of this—which is perhaps the most profound and miraculous of all the wonders this world has to offer—bit through the veneer of sophistry and shrewd argumentation with which the Priest had armed himself and covered himself since his own childhood, and biting through this, touched for a moment the soul of the man underneath. Thereby, the man waited for a certain answer, and was not too surprised when it came.

"I don't want a priest," Madeiros said slowly, organizing his words and his thoughts with great difficulty and great earnestness, "because he may bring fear with him. I am not afraid now. All day long today and yesterday and the day before yesterday and the day before that, I was afraid. I died again and again, and each time I died, I suffered a lot. That fear is the most terrible thing in the world. But now I have here two comrades whose names are Nicola Sacco and Bartolomeo Vanzetti, and they spoke to me and took away my fear. That is why I don't need a priest. If I am not afraid to die, then I am not afraid of anything that comes after death."

"What could they tell you?" the Priest asked desperately. "Can they give you God's absolution?"

"They gave me man's absolution," Madeiros answered as simply as a child.

"Will you pray with me?" the Priest asked.

"I have nothing to pray for," Madeiros answered. "I have found two friends, and they will be with me as long as I am here on this earth."

And with that, he stretched out on his bed, his hands folded beneath his head and his eyes closed—nor did the Priest have the courage to speak to him again. As they had come, so did they go; but this time, as the Priest passed the cells of Sacco and Vanzetti, he looked into them, and he saw in them the men who had become a new legend of New England. And as he looked at them, each of these men looked up in turn, and met his glance with theirs.

Now the Priest walked more quickly through the tunnels and corridors of the State Prison—yet as quickly as he walked, he was able to control himself to a point where the Warden would not know that he was indeed in flight. Beyond him and behind him, in the death house, was a mystery which not only defied his understanding, but threatened his very existence, and now he fled from this mystery.

Chapter 17

THE WARDEN was pleased to be rid of the Priest finally, for so much remained to be done, and here it was already almost ten o'clock. People did not realize how much there was to an execution beyond its factual horror; and sometimes when he was in the mood to philosophize—as what prison warden isn't?—this Warden would contemplate the similarities between his own functions and those of the director of a large and complex funeral establishment. Well, so it was, and it was not any of his doing, and if ending life was surrounded with more ritual than beginning the process, he was not the one who could change this or resist it.

First, the Warden went to the mess hall adjoining the death house, for he had allocated this dining room to the press. It was already filled with a full complement of those reporters who had received special invitations either to witness the execution directly, or to be close at hand if and when it took place. The Warden knew the value of proper press relations, and he had attempted to anticipate all the wants of the reporters and to provide for these wants. The smell of fresh coffee filled the air of the mess hall, and there were piles of appetizing sandwiches and good, fresh coffee cake. The Warden had made a special purchase of twenty-five pounds of delectable cold cuts; for he felt that while there was a need to impress upon anyone who broke bread within the prison that such bread was not worm-eaten, to satisfy so many of the press at one time was even more important.

The telephone company had been equally cooperative, and six branch lines had been installed here, that the news of the details of the execution might go out without impediment or delay to a waiting world. And the Warden had seen to it that there were sufficient yellow copy paper and pencils for any thoughts or fancies the newspaper men might wish to express. It was with some sense of irony that he reflected upon the circumstances which had brought him, his prison, and this particular spot of old Massachusetts, into the focus of all the world's attention; but once again he accepted a situation that was not of his making, and decided that the best thing anyone could do under such circumstances, was to see that everything went smoothly and without untoward incident or complication.

When he appeared in the dining room, the reporters surrounded him and plied him with questions. They wanted all the details which he could provide—the names of the guards and attendants, the name of the prison doctor, the name of everyone else who would be associated with the execution. They also asked him whether he would be in touch with the Governor's office during the last moments before the execution—to make absolutely certain that a postponement would not come a fraction of a minute too late to save the lives of the condemned men. They also wanted to know what the order of the executions would be.

"Gentlemen, gentlemen," the Warden protested. "I would have to spend the whole night here with you to answer all these questions, and there's still a great deal that has to be done. Now I have assigned one of my assistants here to be at your service and to give you all the information that I myself would be able to provide for you. You must understand that we are simply public servants who are given a very unpleasant duty to fulfill. I am not a judge or a policeman, but only the warden of this prison. Of course, I shall make every attempt to be in constant touch with the Governor. You must understand that I have come to know these men, and shall do all I can that might help them with just and legal aid. Now, as far as the order of execution is concerned, we have determined it in this way. The first to die will be Celestino Madeiros. After him, Nicola Sacco, and then finally, Bartolomeo Vanzetti. There you are, gentlemen, and that's the best I can do for you."

They thanked him profusely, and he was not a little proud of the expert and unperturbed manner in which he had dealt with the situation, making neither too much nor too little of it. While the Warden was thus occupied with the press in the mess hall, the prison doctor, the electrician, two guards and the prison barber had come to the death house. Like the Warden, they were painfully aware of the significance of each move they made; but unlike the Warden, it was theirs to deal not with the press, but with the three doomed men in person—and thereby, it was only to be expected that they would shrink from the unpleasant tasks which had been set out for them. Along with this feeling of shame and unhappiness, perhaps to bolster themselves, they inflated their own importance in so enormous an event, and speculated on how they themselves would describe it the following day. Each of them, however, felt personally embarrassed, and personally felt the need to apologize to the three men, the two anarchists and the thief. The barber made his apologies as he shaved their heads.

"You know," he said to Vanzetti, "it is my miserable misfortune to have this job in this place. What can I do about it?"

"There is nothing you can do," Vanzetti answered him, a note of reassurance in his voice. "It's your job and you do it. What else is there to say?"

"I wish I could say something that would help a little bit," the barber insisted. And when he had finished with Vanzetti, he whispered to the electrician that the experience was not as bad as it might have been, and that the man Vanzetti was unquestionably a most unusual and discerning man.

But Sacco said nothing at all, not a word, and when the barber made a few attempts at conversation, Sacco looked up at him in a strange way, and then the barber's words died still-born in his throat.

With Madeiros, the barber had another feeling entirely. Madeiros was like a small boy, and his tranquility became almost terrifying to the barber. Outside in the corridor, he whispered to the guards concerning his tranquility; but they shrugged and dismissed Madeiros as a "hophead," nodding significantly at the door to the execution chamber.

The electrician watched the guards exchange the prisoners' underwear for that special underwear which is made only for such occasions. And the condemned men put on, then, the black suits of death, garments which they would wear for that short distance between the three cells and the electric chair itself; and while he was drawing this horrible suit onto his body, Vanzetti said softly,

"So the bridegroom is dressed! A thoughtful State gives me warm clothes, and the deft hands of a barber to shave me. And strangely enough, fear has gone away. All I feel now is hatred."

He spoke in Italian, and the guards did not know what he was saying; but the barber understood, and whispered a translation of his words to the prison doctor, who shrugged it off with the professional cynicism that such a man must needs arm himself with.

It was the task of the electrician to slit the trouser legs and the sleeves of the death costumes. He did this sullenly, cursing himself and the fate that had brought here to such work. And once, when he touched Vanzetti's flesh, Vanzetti pulled away from him, looking at him with contempt, and then raising his eyes with the same contemptuous hatred to the guards who watched the work of the electrician.

"And this is a service," Vanzetti said, his voice hard and flat as a file. "You lend yourselves to this, and in every age there will be more like you. Even if there were a God, he would not have mercy on the eunuchs who become the handmaidens of death. The truth is that all I wanted was to finish fighting, and instead, the likes of you are reserved to me. But now keep your damned hands away from me! Your hands are dirty with the dirt of the master you serve!"

Again, the barber translated, but the prison doctor said, "Well, what do you expect? You can't do more to anyone than kill him. If he wants to talk, you can't keep him from talking, can you? Don't come to me with any more stories about what he says. He can say what he wants to say."

The guards locked the cell doors once again, and in each cell there was a man clad in black. Not in any way had Madeiros changed. In his black clothes, he sat as calmly on his bed as he had sat before; but Nicola Sacco stood in his cell, plucking at the new garments he wore, and looking at them strangely. Vanzetti, however, remained close to the door, his face framed in the opening. There was anger on his face, and the blood pulsed in his veins with a hard, steady beat. Life coursed through him. He was full of life, vital with it, and the muscles of his arms tensed and hardened as he pulled at the door. He reclaimed the passages of his life without regret, without sorrow, but with a hardening and mounting anger. He saw himself living his free and happy childhood in an Italian village, a place bathed all over with the glow of sunshine. He greeted his mother again, and felt the warm, soft flesh of her face pressed against his own face as she embraced him. He saw her sick and fading while he crouched beside her, never leaving her bedside, trying to pour some of his own vast store of life current into her. Even then, so long ago, he was beginning to have an understanding of these great forces for life and struggle that were lodged within

240

himself. He was like a well, out of which you could dip water endlessly and drink and drink until the thirst of all around was satisfied—yet his own thirst was never quenched.

Italy died with his mother. He saw himself in flight from the old, bucolic life that he had built around her presence. Toil and struggle—work for the dry bread of life, and a savage hunger within him to consume it; that became Bartolomeo Vanzetti, his life, his existence, and the deep meaning of his existence. He was not like Sacco. He was a man born for the troubles and stormy waters of existence—but he was also born to survive them. Now he could not surrender. His whole body screamed to him that surrender was impossible, just as death was impossible and unacceptable—that there had to be a way out, another step forward, another word spoken, another challenge flung! Life was the answer to life; death was not the answer to life. Death was a monster, the dirty, dark and frightful god that his enemies worshipped. He defied death with hatred, with anger, with rage. Life was joined to him—and by the same token, he was joined to life. And now his words and his thoughts were identical.

"I must live—do you understand? I must live! My work has only begun. The fight goes on. I must live and be a part of it. I will not die! I cannot die. . . ."

The prison doctor reported to the Warden in the press room, and the Warden stood up on one of the dining room tables and called for attention and silence from the vast throng of special reporters, newspaper men and columnists who had gathered there.

"As the matter now stands, gentlemen," the Warden said, "we have prepared the prisoners for the execution. That is,

241

the customary procedure of changing their clothes and pre-paring their tonsures has been followed. Only a few min-utes more than an hour remains before the time which the Governor of this State set for their death, a time beginning at midnight. In the hour between eleven o'clock and mid-night, we shall have to test the wiring which will bear the load of electricity. If in that time you see the lights of the prison dim suddenly, you will know that this test is being made. I shall now go to my office and call the Governor, and also arrange for any messages from the Governor to be delivered to me immediately."

arms, and the men are marked all over with toil and the hours they have worked. There must be some particular quality in their grief to have brought them here to this doleful march. What can it be? What do they think?" And then he added to himself, "It's strange, but never in all my life have I concerned myself with what such men and women think. Now I want to know. I want to know what special bond ties them together with Sacco and Vanzetti; I want to know what makes me afraid."

For the truth of it was that his fear had more sources than one and more directions than one. The awful chill of death crept around his heart when he thought of what faced Sacco and Vanzetti in so short a time; but still another chill of fear and foreboding touched him when he contemplated the set and somber and angry faces of the people on the picket line. Then he could not help but think to himself,

"What if they should wake up? These and the millions more—what if they should wake up and say that Sacco and Vanzetti shall not die? What then? Where do I stand?"

There was no denying that he was very deeply troubled. Earlier on this very day, at the Defense Headquarters, he had expressed this sense of doubt and deep concern to a representative of the International Labor Defense, a man he knew to be a communist. A tall, angular, red-headed man, slow of speech, a one-time lumberjack in the Northwest, he had been elected to his state legislature on the Socialist ticket, and a few years later had become a charter member of the newly formed left-Socialist or Communist Party. He made no secret of it—and partly for that reason, the Professor of Criminal Law had sought him out earlier this evening and spoke to him out of his lowest moment of despair.

"Now they will die, and there is no hope left."

"As long as time is left, hope is left," the Communist answered.

"An answer by rote," the Professor said, his voice bitter. "I have been to the prison and come back from there. It is the end, and as hopeless at the end as it was at the beginning. I am sick with it. I know the men are guiltless, and yet they must die. My faith in human decency will die with them."

"Your faith dies easily," the Communist said.

"Does it? Is your faith stronger? Where is your faith, sir?"

"With the working people of America," the Communist answered.

"That's a lesson you've learned, but isn't it at odds with reality? I've never argued with you people. I've known you were everywhere around this case, and sometimes I've even admired the energy and the selflessness with which you worked. I would not permit myself to redbait, as others do, for in my own way I have as great a necessity as anyone to live in a world where justice prevails. For that reason, I worked with you, but now your position angers me. What faith in the working people? Where are they? Oh, I agree that Sacco and Vanzetti are being put to death because they are working men, Italians, communists, agitators—because a scapegoat is needed, an example, a warning. But where are your working people? The Federation does nothing, and the great Federation leaders sit at home—they are not even on the picket line. And the working men—where are they?"

"Everywhere."

"Is that an answer?"

"For the moment, it is. What would you want—for the working people to storm the jail and free Sacco and Vanzetti? Things are not done that way—except in foolish dreams. They may kill Sacco and Vanzetti; they killed Albert Parsons, and Tom Mooney is in jail, and there will be others too, but not forever. They do these murderous things only for one reason—because they fear us, and they know we will not endure these things forever."

"Who? The communists?"

"No, not the communists. The working people. And those who murder Sacco and Vanzetti hate the communists only because the communists are knit to the working people."

"What notions you have!" the Professor said. "Would you want me to believe this tonight—of all nights?"

"You can't believe it. For you, when Sacco and Vanzetti die, there will die with them all hopes and dreams of justice and reason."

"That's a cruel thing to say."

"But admit that it's the truth."

"And if I do? Don't you talk too glibly of opposing a power as great as this? The whole world cries out that they shall not die, and yet they will die. I admit I am afraid. I put my faith in something, and it's lost. I don't know your nameless working people. I don't understand them—any more than I understand you."

"Any more than you understand Sacco and Vanzetti?"

251

"Any more than I understand Sacco and Vanzetti," the Professor of Criminal Law admitted sadly. And there was truth in this; his grief was in good measure for his own shattered hopes and lost faith, and walking on the picket line, he said to himself,

"Now indeed do I weep for myself and not for them. Something most precious and irreplaceable within me is going to die, and I weep because I am the chief mourner."

So each wept in his own fashion—but there were some who remained dry-eyed; and these dry-eyed ones did other things instead of weeping. They pledged to themselves a long memory and an absolute identification. They made notations in their own hearts and they drew up a balance sheet that extended as far back as the memory of mankind and the first whiplash on the first bent back. These dry-eyed ones said to themselves, "There is a better way than weeping and a better way than tears."

And now in the prison itself, the final hour came to its finish, and the moment arrived for the first of the three men to die. That was Celestino Madeiros, thief and murderer, and the deputy warden of the prison and two prison guards came to his cell and beckoned to him. Madeiros had been waiting for them, and very quietly and with amazing dignity, he took his place between the two guards and walked with them for the thirteen paces that separated his cell from the execution chamber. When he entered this chamber, he stopped for a moment and let his eyes travel over the faces of the assembled spectators. Afterwards, some said that a look of anger passed across his face, but more of those who watched him agreed that he was unmoved and unperturbed as he sat down in the electric chair. The signal was given, and two thousand volts of electricity were sent coursing through his body. The lights of the prison grew dim and then strong again, and Celestino Madeiros was dead.

The second to die was Nicola Sacco. Like Madeiros, he walked with a simple dignity which, coming after the behavior of the first doomed man, sent chills of fear through the spectators. It was neither normal nor reasonable that two men should go to their death in this fashion, yet here it was happening.

Sacco said never a word. With great calm and dignity, he walked to the electric chair and sat down. He looked straight ahead of him while they fastened the electrodes. The lights dimmed, and a moment later, Nicola Sacco was dead.

The last of the three was Bartolomeo Vanzetti. Now the procedure had become a challenge to the officials and the representatives of the press who were there to observe and to write about the execution. After the silence which had accompanied the death of Sacco, there was an audible sigh that went up from the crowd, and then there was a whispering back and forth as to what Vanzetti would do. They whispered in order to prepare themselves for his entrance into the death chamber, but whisper though they might, they could not prepare themselves wholly or properly. They could not anticipate the lion-like poise of him as he walked into the execution chamber, or the dignity with which he stood before them. His self-possession, his calm, his command of the situation, was more than they could bear, callous though they were, and armed as they were with the fortitude required to witness a triple execution.

He broke through their defenses. He looked at them with what can only be described as a sense of judgment, and he pronounced the words he had decided to say, slowly and clearly.

"I wish to say to you," Vanzetti told them, "that I am innocent. I have never committed any crime—some sins—but never any crime. . . ."

There were hard men there, but hard as they were, their throats constricted, and many among them began to cry silently. It never occurred to them to halt their tears now with the argument that they were only weeping for two Italian radicals who were supposedly alien to all that is known as Americanism. This never occurred to them. Some of them closed their eyes, and others turned their heads away—and then the lights waned, and when the lights became bright again, Bartolomeo Vanzetti was dead.

Epilogue

At that time, in the city of Boston, there was a club known as the Athenaeum, and to this club there belonged those whose names were connected with the city's past, with the long past days of Emerson and Thoreau. Such men as the President of the University, who sat in final judgment on Sacco and Vanzetti, were powerful influences in this club—a place into which no foreigner, no first-generation upstart, no Jew or Negro, had ever penetrated.

On the morning after the execution, on August 23, 1927, a slip of paper was found to have been inserted in every magazine in the reading room of the club. And on each slip of paper were the following words:

"On this day, Nicola Sacco and Bartolomeo Vanzetti, dreamers of the brotherhood of man, who hoped it might be found in America, were done to a cruel death by the children of those who fled long ago to this land of hope and freedom."